Edward Spangler

Testimony for Prosecution and Defence in the Case of

Edward Spangler

tried for conspiracy to murder the President, before a military

commission, of which Major-General Hunter was president, Washington,

D.C., May and June, 1865

Edward Spangler

Testimony for Prosecution and Defence in the Case of Edward Spangler
tried for conspiracy to murder the President, before a military commission, of which
Major-General Hunter was president, Washington, D.C., May and June, 1865

ISBN/EAN: 9783337367756

Printed in Europe, USA, Canada, Australia, Japan

Cover: Foto ©Andreas Hilbeck / pixelio.de

More available books at **www.hansebooks.com**

TESTIMONY FOR PROSECUTION AND DEFENCE

IN THE CASE OF

EDWARD SPANGLER,

Tried for Conspiracy to Murder the President,

BEFORE A

MILITARY COMMISSION, OF WHICH MAJOR-GENERAL HUNTER WAS PRESIDENT, WASHINGTON, D. C., MAY AND JUNE, 1865.

THOMAS EWING, Jr., Counsel for the Accused.

MAY 17.

SERGEANT JOSEPH M. DYE,

a witness called for the prosecution, being duly sworn, testified as follows :

By the JUDGE ADVOCATE:

Q. State whether or not, on the evening of the 14th of April last, you were in front of Ford's Theatre, and at what hour you were there.

A. I was sitting in front of Ford's Theatre about half-past nine o'clock.

Q. Did you observe several persons, whose appearance excited your suspicions, conferring together upon the pavement in front of the theatre?

A. Yes, sir.

Q. Describe their appearance, and what they did.

A. The first appearance was an elegantly dressed gentleman, who came out of the passage, and commenced conversing with a ruffianly-looking fellow. Then there was another one appeared, and the three conversed together. After they had conversed together, it was drawing near the second act. The one that appeared to be the leader of them, the well-dressed one, said, "I think he will come out now," referring to the President, I supposed.

Q. Was the President's carriage standing there?

A. Yes, sir. One of them had been standing out, looking at the carriage on the curbstone, while I was sitting there, and then went back. They watched a while, and the rush came down; many gentlemen came out and went in and had a drink in the saloon below. Then, after they went up, the best-dressed gentleman stepped into the saloon himself; remained there long enough to get a drink, and came out in a style as if he was becoming intoxicated. He stepped up and whispered to this ruffian, (that is, the miserablest-looking one of the three,) and stepped into the passage—the passage that leads to the stage there from the street. Then the smallest one stepped up and called the time, just as the best dressed gentleman appeared again, from the clock in the vestibule. Then he started up the street, and remained there a while, and came down again, and called the time again. Then I began to think there was something going on, and looked towards this man as he called the time. Presently he went up again, and came down then and called the time again. Then I began to think there was something going on, and I looked towards the man as he called the time. Presently he went up again, and then came down and called the time louder. I think it was ten minutes after ten that he called out then.

Q. Was he announcing it to the other two?

A. Yes, sir; then he started on a fast walk up the street, and the best-dressed one among them started into the theatre, and went inside; I was invited by Sergeant Cooper to have some oysters, and we had barely time to get in the saloon and get seated, and order the oysters, when a man came running in and said the President was shot.

Q. Would you recognize that well-dressed person from his photograph, if you were to see it now?

A. Yes, sir.

Q. [Exhibiting Booth's photograph, Exhibit No. 1] Look at that photograph.

A. That was the man ; but his moustache was heavier and his hair longer than in this picture.

Q. But do you recognize the features ?

A. Yes, sir ; this is the man ; these are his features exactly.

Q. What restaurant did that man go into to drink?

A. The restaurant just below the theatre, towards the avenue.

Q. Did he go in alone?

A. Yes, sir; he went in alone.

Q. Can you give a more particular description of the ruffianly-looking man whom you saw? What was his size? and what was it that gave him such a ruffianly appearance? Was it his dress?

A. He was not as well dressed as the rest of them.

Q. Was he shabbily dressed or dirtily dressed?

A. His clothes had been worn a considerable time, and he had a bloated appearance.

Q. Was he a stout man?

A. Yes, sir, and a rough face.

Q. Which way did he go?

A. He remained there at the passage, and the other one started up the street.

Q. The time was announced to the other two men three times by him, was it?

A. Yes, sir, three times.

Q. The last, you think, was ten minutes after ten?

A. The last time he called out was ten minutes after ten.

Q. Immediately on announcing that, did Booth leave and go into the theatre?

A. He whispered to the ruffian and started in.

Q. Look at these prisoners and see whether you recognize any of them as either of the persons present on that occasion?

A. If that man [pointing to Edw'd Spangler] had a moustache, it would be just the appearance of the face exactly.

Q. Do you mean that the rough looking man was like him, except that he had a moustache?

A. Yes, sir. He was standing at the entrance of the passage, but I think he had a moustache, a heavy one. It was rather dark back there; the gas-light did not shine very much on it, but I saw the moustache.

Q. I understand you to state that the call was made from the clock in the ball of the theatre?

A. Yes, sir. He stepped up there and called the time right in front of the theatre.

Q. Can you tell at what time the other calls were made? You have stated that the last was at ten minutes past ten.

A. They were all between half-past nine and ten minutes after ten.

Q. Do you think you could recognize either of the other persons?

A. The one that called the time was a very neat gentleman, well-dressed and he had a moustache.

Q. Do you see him here?

A. He was better dressed than any I see here. He had on one of the fashionable hats

they wear here in Washington, with round tops and stiff brim.

Q. Can you describe his dress as to color and appearance?

A. No, sir, I cannot exactly describe it.

Q. How was the well-dressed man as to size?

A. He was not a very large man—about five feet six inches high.

Q. You have never seen that man before or since?

A. No, sir.

Q. Do you remember the color of that man's clotnes?

A. His coat was a kind of drab color.

Q. What color was his hat?

A. His hat was black, similar to the one I had on the same night.

Q. Did you observe whether they had spurs on, any of them?

A. I did not observe that.

Cross-examined by Mr. AIKEN:

Q. You say that the well-dressed man wore a black hat, and was about five feet six inches high?

A. Yes, sir.

Cross-examined by Mr. EWING:

Q. How long did you observe the slouchy man?

A. I observed him while I was sitting there.

Q. About how long?

A. While I was sitting there and until I left.

Q. Could you not fix some time?

A. I was there till the last time was called, and I was there from about twenty-five minutes after nine or half-past nine.

Q. You went there at twenty-five minutes after nine or half-past nine, and left when this man called, ten minutes past ten?

A. Yes, sir.

Q. Was the slouchy man there during the whole of that time—the man dressed in slouched clothes?

A. Yes, sir; he remained at the passage.

Q. Was he there during the whole of that time?

A. Yes, sir.

Q. Will you describe the several articles of his dress as near as you can?

A. I could not observe him well; he was back, and it was rather dark there.

Q. Could you see his countenance?

A. Yes, sir.

Q. Did you notice the color of his eyes?

A. No, sir; I did not observe that.

Q. Did you notice the color of his moustache?

A. The moustache was black.

Q. Did you notice the color of his hair?

A. No, sir; because he remained in one position.

Q. What shaped hat had he on?

A. A slouched hat; one that had been worn some time.

Q. Had he an overcoat on?

A. I did not observe that.

Q. Do you recollect anything as to the color of the coat?

A. No, sir; he did not move around, and I did not pay any particular attention, only that I observed the well-dressed gentleman would whisper to him; that was all.

Q. Exactly where did he stand?

A. Right at the passage.

Q. Inside?

A. No, sir; right at the end of the passage.

Q. On the pavement?

A. Yes, sir.

Q. Near the President's carriage?

A. No, sir; the President's carriage was at the curb-stone.

Q. Did he occupy the same position during the whole of this time?

A. That man did.

Q. You refer to the man of slouched dress?

A. Yes, sir.

Q. Which way did Booth enter the last time?

A. He just stepped right up into the front door.

Q. Did you see the man in slouched dress standing there at that time?

A. When Booth whispered to him and left him, I did not see him change his position, because I was observing Booth. As soon as Booth stepped into the theatre, we started. The other man started on a fast walk up the street.

Q. You do not know whether the man in the slouched dress did not come out on the pavement before Booth went out?

A. I do not recollect his coming out on the pavement.

Q. What attracted your attention to that man?

A. This elegantly-dressed, gentlemanly-looking man addressing him.

Q. When did you notice him speak to him first?

A. When I first came there.

Q. At about twenty-five minutes past nine or half-past nine?

A. Yes, sir.'

Q. How long after Booth entered the theatre was it that you heard the news of the assassination?

A. I cannot state the precise time.

Q. About what time?

A. Well, fifteen minutes, I presume.

Q. Do you think it was as long as that?

A. It might not have been as long, but I cannot be certain.

Q. What did you do in the meantime?

A. We started, turned the corner, went into a saloon; debated a while which saloon to go to. I do not know how long it took us. We had just got in and ordered oysters, as a man came in telling us the news.

Q. Do you think it was not exceeding fifteen minutes?

A. I think so.

Q. Do you think it may have been less?

A. I do not know about that; I am not certain.

Q. About how high do you think the man dressed in the slouched clothes was?

A. He was about five feet eight or nine inches.

By Mr. Aiken:

Q. Will you state, as near as you can recollect, the time you first observed those gentlemen in front of the theatre?

A. Twenty-five minutes or half-after nine o'clock.

By the Court:

Q. Do you say, without hesitation, that Spangler was the man?

A. I say that was the countenance, except the moustache.

Q. Do you say that was the man?

A. I say the countenance was the same; he resembled that face as much as possible.

By Mr. Ewing:

Q. Have you seen this man since the assassination of the President?

A. Yes, sir.

Q. Where?

A. In the Capitol Prison.

Q. In the presence of what persons?

A. In the presence of the proprietor, I presume, Sergeant Cooper, and another prisoner.

Q. Did it seem to you then that he was the man?

A. All but the moustache.

Q. But you say that he was under the shadow, so that you could not observe his features distinctly?

A. I remember the face—the expression of his countenance.

Q. But you did not see his eyes?

A. No, sir.

JOHN E. BUCKINGHAM,

a witness called for the prosecution, being duly sworn, testified as follows:

By the Judge Advocate:

Q. Do you reside in Washington?

A. Yes, sir.

Q. What business were you engaged in during the month of October?

A. I am at night doorkeeper at Mr. Ford's Theatre, and in the daytime I am employed in the Washington Navy Yard.

Q. Were you acquainted with J. Wilkes Booth during his lifetime?

A. Yes, sir; I knew him by coming to the theatre.

Q. You knew him by sight?

A. Yes, sir.

Q. Will you state whether or not you saw him on the evening of the 14th of April, at what hour, and what occurred in connection with it?

A. I should judge it was about ten o'clock

that he came there to the theatre, walked in, and walked out again, and he returned, I judge, in about two or three minutes. He came to me and asked me what time it was. I told him to step into the lobby that leads out into the street, and he could see. He stepped out, and walked in again and stepped into the door that leads to the parquette and dress circle, and returned immediately, came out, and went up the stairway to the dress circle. The last I saw of him was, he alighted on the stage from the box, running across the stage with a knife in his hand. He was uttering some sentence, but I could not understand it well at the time; I was too far back from him, at the front door.

Q. He went into the President's box, did he?

A. I could not say.

Q. He was on that side of the dress circle?

A. I was down below, underneath. The dress circle extends over my doorway, so that I could not see.

Cross-examined by Mr. Ewing:

Q. Are you acquainted with the prisoner, Edward Spangler?

A. Yes, sir; knowing him at the theatre.

Q. You have known him?

A. I have known him to be there at the theatre.

Q. Did you see him enter or come out of the front of the theatre during the play?

A. I did not.

Q. State the position of your box. Is it that you would be likely to see any persons who entered from the front of the theatre?

A. Yes, sir; every person has to pass me on entering the theatre; that is, in the lower part, for the parquette, dress circle, and orchestra.

Q. Do you observe the persons that go in?

A. No, I do not take notice of the persons.

Q. Do you see that persons do not go in who are not authorized to do so?

A. Yes, sir.

Q. If this man Spangler had gone in from the street, entering at the front of the theatre, would you likely have seen him?

A. Yes, sir.

Q. Would you have been pretty sure to see him?

A. Yes, sir, he could not have passed me without my seeing him.

Q. Are you certain he did not pass then?

A. I am perfectly satisfied that he was not in the front part of the house that night.

Q. Did you see him that night at all?

A. Not to my recollection.

Q. Did you ever see him wear a moustache?

A. No, sir, not as I can recollect of.

JAMES P. FERGUSON,

a witness called for the prosecution, being duly sworn, testified as follows:

By the JUDGE ADVOCATE:

Q. Do you reside in Washington city?

A. Yes, sir.

Q. What business are you engaged in?

A. The restaurant business.

Q. Where?

A. No. 452 Tenth street.

Q. Near Ford's Theatre?

A. Adjoining the theatre, on the upper side.

Q. Did you know J. Wilkes Booth in his lifetime?

A. I did.

Q. Did you see him on that evening?

A. I saw him that afternoon; I do not recollect exactly what time, but it was some time between two and four o'clock, I think. He came up in front, just below my door, on the street. I walked out to the door and saw Mr. Maddox standing out by the side of his horse—a small bay mare. Mr. Maddox was standing aside of him, with his hand on the horse's mane, talking. I stood on the porch a minute, and Booth looked around and said, "See what a nice horse I have got." As I stepped out near him, he said, "Now watch; he can run just like a cat;" and struck his spurs into the horse, and off he went down the street. I did not see him any more until that night, somewhere near ten o'clock, I should think. Along in the afternoon, about one o'clock, Harry Ford came into my place and said to me, "Your favorite, General Grant, is going to be in the theatre to-night, and if you want to see him, you had better go and get a seat." I went and secured a seat directly opposite the President's box, in the front of the dress circle. He showed me the box that he said the President was to be in, and I got those seats directly opposite. I saw the President and his family when they came in, and some gentleman in plain clothes with them. I did not recognize him, but I knew from the appearance of the man that it was not Grant. I supposed that probably Grant had remained outside so as not to create any excitement in the theatre, and would come in alone and come in the box; and I made up my mind that I would see him before he went in, and I watched every one that passed around on that side of the dress circle toward this box. Somewhere near ten o'clock, I should think it was—it was the second scene in the third act of the play they were playing—Our American Cousin—I saw Booth pass along near the box, and then stop and lean against the wall. He stood there a moment. Something directed my attention on the stage, and I looked back and saw him step down one step, put his hands to the door and his knee against it, and push the door open—the first door that goes into the box. I did not see any more of him until I saw him make a rush for the railings that ran around the box to jump over. I saw him put his left hand on the railing, and he seemed to strike back with the right with a knife. I could see the knife gleam, and that moment he was over the box. The President sat in the left-hand corner of the box, and Miss Harris in the right-hand corner. Mrs. Lincoln sat to the right of the President, as I am sitting here. Then the gentleman in citizen's clothes, whom I learned afterward was Major Rathbone, sat back almost in the corner of the box. The President, at the time he was shot, was sitting in this position; he was leaning his hand on the rail, and was looking down at a person in the orchestra, not looking on the stage. He had the flag that decorated the box pulled around, and was looking between the post and the flag. As the person lit on the stage, just as he jumped over, I saw it was Booth. I saw the flash of the pistol back right in the box. As he struck on the stage, he rose and exclaimed, "Sic semper tyrannis," and ran right directly across the stage to the opposite door, where the actors come in. I did not see anything more of him that evening. I got out as quick as I could. I had a little girl with me, who lived on E street. As I understood General Grant was to be at the theatre that night, I took her with me to see him. I got her home as quick as I could, and then ran down Ninth street to D, and through D to the police station, went up stairs, and told the Superintendent of Police, Mr. Webb. I then ran up Tenth street to the house where the President was. Some one told me that General Augur was up there, or Colonel Wells. Colonel Wells was standing out on the step of Mr. Peterson's house. I told him I had seen it all, and knew the man that jumped out of the box. He told the guard to pass me through, and I went in and stated it to him. I then went over the street and went to bed. In the morning, when I got up, I saw Mr. Gifford, and he said to me, "You made a hell of a statement about what you saw last night. How could you see the flash of the pistol when the ball was shot through the door?" I said to him, "Mr. Gifford, that pistol never exploded in any place but in the box; I saw the flash." Said he, "Oh, hell, the ball was shot through the door, and how could you see it?" I studied about it all day. On Sunday morning, Miss Harris came down, and her father, Senator Harris, and Judge Olin and Judge Carter, and I went into the theatre with them. We had a great deal of difficulty in getting the theatre open. Maddox and Gifford were in the theatre, but would not open the door. I sent a young man through my back way, and he broke a window in, and then Maddox came to the front door, opened the theatre, and let us in. We got a candle and examined this hole, where Mr. Gifford said the ball was shot through. It looked to me like as if it had been bored by a small gimlet, and then cut around the edge with a knife; and in several places it was scratched

down as if with a knife. This thing had bothered me all night on Saturday night, and after this examination, I was satisfied that I saw the flash of the pistol. Mr. Gifford's accusing me of making this statement bothered me all night. I saw him on Monday, and said to him, "Mr. Gifford, you are a very smart man. You knew that ball was not shot through the board." Said he, "I have understood since that it was cut through." Said I, "Did you not know it was cut through?" Said he, "No; how did I know anything about it?" and walked away and left me.

Q. Is Gifford the chief carpenter of the theatre?

A. Yes, sir; he had charge of the theatre altogether. He was chief carpenter, and then he had the management of the theatre; he had full charge of it; at least, I always understood so. I recollect that when Richmond was surrendered, I mentioned to him, "Have you not got any flags in the theatre?" He said to me, "Yes, I have; I guess there is a flag about." I said to him, "Why do you not run it out on that roof?" and he said, "There is a rope; is not that enough?" Said I, "You are a hell of a man; you ought to be in the Old Capitol," and walked away and left him. He did not like me anyhow.

Q. The President's box was on the south side of the theatre?

A. Yes, sir; he always had that box every time I ever saw him at the theatre.

Q. Did you hear any other exclamation besides "Sic Semper Tyrannis?"

A. I heard some one hallo out of the box—I do not know that it was him; I suppose it was though; it must have been—"Revenge for the South," just as he was putting his foot over this railing. There was a post there, and the President was right in the corner, and he jumped in between the President and the post. Just as he went over the box, I saw the President raise his head and then it hung back, and I saw Mrs. Lincoln catch him on the arm. I was satisfied then that he was hurt. By that time Booth was across the stage.

Q. Did Booth's spur catch in the flag?

A. His spur caught in the flag that was stretched around the box. There was also a flag decorating this post. His spur caught in the blue part of it. I thought it was a State flag at first by the looks of it, but I saw afterwards when I examined it that it was the blue part of the American flag. As he went over, his spur caught in the moulding that ran around the edge of the box and also in this flag, and tore a piece of the flag as he struck on the stage, and it was dragged half-way across the stage on his spur. I saw that the spur was on his right heel.

Q. Did you observe that hole closely to see whether it had been freshly cut?

A. No, sir; I could not tell; it looked as

though it was just done. Miss Harris remarked that morning, "There is one thing I want to examine; I am satisfied there was a bar across the door when I jumped off my seat and called for assistance." We went and looked, and there was a square hole cut in the wall just big enough to let in a bar, and this ran across to the door. The door stands in a kind of an angle, and this bar being placed in the wall, the other end came against the door, and you could not open it. That had been cut with a penknife, as it looked to me. There was a scratch down the wall.

Q. Could you observe the character of the spur at all, or did he move too rapidly for that?

A. I could not observe that. The way I noticed the spur was, when I saw the flag pulled down I watched to see what it was caught to, as he went over the edge of the box.

Q. You did not see him after he disappeared behind the scenes?

A. No, sir; I did not see him afterwards. He ran right across the stage. I was up in the dress-circle and he ran out the side door. A young man named Hawk was the only one on the stage at the time. As he went over he had the knife raised, the handle up and the blade down.

Q. He went out on the opposite corner of the stage from the President's box?

A. Yes, sir; he ran right straight across the stage.

Cross-examined by Mr. Ewing:

Q. Did you see the bar?

A. I did not. We could not find it. There was no bar there on Sunday morning.

Q. Do you know Edward Spangler, the prisoner at the bar?

A. I know Mr. Spangler.

Q. Did you see him that night?

A. I do not recollect seeing him that night at all. I was in the theatre all the night. I went in, I think, at about twenty minutes to eight o'clock. I wanted to be there before the party came there, and I went in early. I did not see Mr. Spangler that night at all, that I recollect.

Q. Do you know him well?

A. Yes, sir; he worked at the theatre,

Q. Did you ever see him wear a moustache?

A. I do not think I ever did. I do not recollect ever seeing him wear a moustache. He never wore any moustache, I think, since I have been there.

WILLIAM WITHERS, JR.

a witness called for the prosecution, being duly sworn, testified as follows:

By the JUDGE ADVOCATE:

Q. Do you belong to the orchestra of Ford's Theatre?

A. Yes, sir.

Q. Were you there on the night of the assassination of the President?

A. Yes, sir.

Q. Did you see J. Wilkes Booth?

A. Yes, sir.

Q. State what you saw of him.

A. I had some business on the stage with our stage manager that night in regard to a national song that I had composed, and I went to see in what costume they were going to sing it in, as it was the after piece. I went up on the stage and talked with the stage manager a little while, and he told me that they would sing it in the costume they wore in the piece. After that was over I went to return under the stage, where my orchestra was, and went very leisurely along, and I heard the report of the pistol just as I was in the act of going under the stage. I stood with astonishment to think why they should fire a pistol off in "Our American Cousin," as I had never heard of such a thing before. As I turned around I heard a confusion, and met this man [Booth] running towards me, with his head down. I stood completely paralyzed at the time. I did not know what was the matter. As he ran I could not get out of his way, so he hit me on the leg and turned me around, and made two cuts at me—one in the neck and one on the side—and knocked me from the third entrance down to the second. The scene saved me. As I turned I got a side view of him, and I saw it was John Wilkes Booth. He then made a rush for the door, and out he went. After that was over I returned on the stage, and I heard then that the President was killed, and I saw him in the box, apparently dead.

Q. Which way did he go out of the theatre?

A. Out of the back door.

Cross-examined by Mr. EWING:

Q. Are you acquainted with the prisoner Edward Spangler?

A. I have known him ever since I have been in the theatre.

Q. Did you see him that night?

A. No sir; I do not recollect of seeing him that night. I only happened to go on the stage in that act that night to see the stage-manager, Mr Wright.

Q. Which side of the stage did you go on?

A. The right hand side facing the audience.

Q. That was the side farthest from the President box?

A. Yes, sir.

Q. What was the position of this man Spangler? What place had he on the stage, if any?

A. His position ought to have been at the scene. If it should be changed, right in the centre of the stage. His business there is to change the scenes, and he ought to have been there, either at the wing or right behind the scenes.

Q. On which side?

A. I really do not know. There are two that shift the scenes, but I do not know which position he had there.

Q. You do not know which side was his position?

A. No, sir.

Q. Do you know whether the passage through which Booth passed out of the door is obstructed generally?

A. Sometimes there are a great many scenes there so that you cannot pass. During some of the pieces while Mr. Forrest was there, there were a great many scenes put up against the wall, and generally there are a lot of tools lying close by this door, but on that night everything seemed to be clear. I met nobody there that night that I met John Wilkes Booth.

Q. Was there a necessity for many shiftings of the scenes in the play that night?

A. There was a very long wait in that scene. I think it was the time Asa Treuchard was to meet Mary Meredith and propose to her. After he does that they both go off and the scene changes there. I do not think it wanted many minutes until the scene changed.

Q. Was it a time in the scene, and such a scene, where the stage and that passage-way would probably, in the ordinary course of things, have been obstructed?

A. A little, by some of the scene-shifters. They might have been there, and the actors; some of them had to go on the next scene, which required their presence.

Q. Where is the actor's room?

A. The actor's room is to the right, facing the audience as you go up the stairs; the green room is about two yards from the stage; there is a wall partition that separated the stage and the green-room, and then there is the stars' room, on the first floor, end up stairs are the dressing-rooms for the actors.

Q. The green-room is the place where the actors wait before going on the stage?

A. Yes, sir; they are called from this room to prepare to go on the stage about five minutes or sometimes two minutes before they go on the stage, and they sit down there and wait for the call-boy to call them and go on in the respective scenes.

Q. Did Booth pass between the scenes and the green room?

A. Yes, sir.

Q. How wide is that passage between the scenes and the green room?

A. I should judge it to be about as wide as this railing, (about four feet.) The door faces right on the stage. There is another scene that comes to separate it, but this leaves the door from the scene. You look from the scenes to the dressing-room. Here is a scene and there also; and from here there is a prompter's desk, and this scene is open from the door that leads into the dressing-room. Then there is an open space that leads right on to the stage, and nothing to obstruct the passage.

Q. I mean from the door out of which he passed?

A. It is not so large as the dressing-room door there, and there are some scenes there that obstruct the passage for anybody.— Where we go down under the stage there is a little box made, where the carpenters put their tools on sometimes. You have to stoop as you go under to get to the orchestra, and there is only a little narrow passage as you get out of this door. It is narrower about two yards before you get to the door than before.

Q. And in passing from where Booth leaped on the stage to where he made his exit, he would leave the green-room to the left?

A. Yes, sir.

Q. As he would pass between the scenes and the green-room?

A. No; he would pass the green-room door. There is a partition that separates the green-room. You have to go in about two yards after leaving this door to get into the green-room, and when that is shut, the stage is all open.

Q. Did you ever see Spangler wear a moustache?

A. No. I have seen him as he appears now. I do not recollect ever seeing him wear a moustache.

Q. How long have you known him?

A. Ever since Ford's Theatre was opened. I played there when it first opened.

Q. How long?

A. That is going on two years now.

By the JUDGE ADVOCATE:

Q. Will you state if there is not a side way by which the theatre can be entered without passing through the door—passing between the saloon and the theatre?

A. Not that I know of.

Q. Cannot it be entered from the street in that way, going in the back way?

A. Not that I know of. There is only one little passage where the actors and the orchestra get in, that leads out of the saloon. There is a door that leads into the saloon, and from this passage leads into the theatre.

Q. That is used by the actors and persons connected with the theatre?

A. Yes, sir. It was used when the theatre first opened, so that the actors could go out, without being observed, to get a drink sometimes. This little door leads into the bar-room.

Q. Is there a passage way from the rear of the theatre to the front without passing through that front door?

A. Not that I know of.

By the COURT:

Q. When you met Booth on the stage as he was passing out, could you see the door where he went out?

A. Yes, sir.

Q. Was there any door-keeper standing around there that you saw?

A. I did not see one.

Q. Was the door open?

A. I do not think it was, because, as I turned around when I heard the report of the pistol—I was astonished that a pistol should be fired off in that piece—I looked at the door, because the door was only a yard from me.

Q. There was nothing to obstruct his passage out?

A. No, sir, nothing.

Q. Was not that an unusual state of things?

A. It seemed strange to me.

Q. Was it not unusual?

A. Yes, sir.

Q. Was there any check at the door, or was it open before?

A. No, sir. When he gave me the blow that knocked me down in the scene, and when I came to and got a side view of him, it seemed to me that he made one plunge at the door, and as soon as he made the plunge he was out.

Q. The door opens out?

A. I think it opens inward on the stage.

Q. Was it your impression that the door was opened for him, or did he open it himself?

A. I do not know.

Q. What was your impression?

A. It seems to me I tried it myself the day I went to rehearsal, to get a hold of the door, because it surprised me that he made a jump and went out of the door.

Q. There was no delay, but he passed right out?

A. There was no delay; from the jump he made he went right out.

Q. Was it your impression that some one assisted him to get out by opening the door?

A. I could not say. I tried the door to see if the knob would come that way. I did not see anybody, only him, go out.

By the Judge Advocate:

Q. Do the scenes stand at this moment just as they were left at that time, or have they been changed?

A. I really do not know.

By the Court:

Q. Did you say there was no way for any person getting out from the rear of the theatre except out of the front entrance?

A. You have to come to the front, without you go to the alley and come in the front.

Joe Simms, (Colored,)

a witness called for the prosecution, being duly sworn, testified as follows:

By the Judge Advocate:

Q. Do you live in this city?

A. Yes, sir.

Q. What connection have you had with Ford's Theatre?

A. I worked there two years. I came there when I first came to Washington.

Q. Were you there on the night the President was assassinated?

A. I was up on the flies, to wind up the curtain.

Q. Did you see Booth there that evening?

A. I saw Mr. Booth that evening between 5 and 6 o'clock.

Q. State where you saw him, and what he did and said.

A. When I saw him, he came in on the back part of the stage, and went through to the front of the house. I was in front of the house, and Mr. Booth came out there and went out and into one of the restaurants by the side of the theatre. I saw him no more that night until the performance was. During the performance, I heard the fire of a pistol, and looked immediately to see where it was. When I looked I saw him jumping out of the private box down on to the stage, with a bowie-knife in his hand, and then making his escape across the stage. I saw no more of him.

Q. Did you hear anything that he said?

A. No, sir; not a word.

Q. Who was with him when he went out to drink?

A. There was nobody with him then; but one of the men, a man named Spangler, was sitting out in front, and he invited him in to take a drink.

Q. Is that the man who is here?

A. That is the man, [pointing to Edward Spangler.]

Q. Did you hear a word said between them?

A. Not a word. They went into the restaurant and took a drink; that was all I saw or heard.

Q. Did you see or hear Booth when he came up to the back of the theatre with his horse?

A. I did not hear him myself, neither did I see him; but the other colored man that works with me saw him.

Q. Is he here?

A. He is here.

Q. You know Mr. Spangler very well?

A. Yes, sir.

Q. Were he and Booth very intimate?

A. They were quite intimate together, but I know not of anything between them.

Q. You only saw them often together?

A. Yes, sir.

Q. Drinking together?

A. Yes, sir.

Cross-examined by Mr. Ewing:

Q. Did Mr. Spangler have anything to do with Booth's horses?

A. No more than he used to have them attended to while Mr. Booth was away.

Q. He had charge of the horses?

A. Yes, sir.

Q. Saw to their being fed and watered?

A. Yes, sir.

Q. Was he hired by Mr. Booth?

A. Mr. Spangler was not, but there was a young man hired by Mr. Booth. I suppose Mr. Booth thought this young man might not do right by his horses, and he got Mr. Spangler to see that it should be done right when he was not there.

Q. What position had Mr. Spangler in the theatre?

A. Mr. Spangler was one of the stage managers, one that shoved the scenes at night and worked on the stage all day.

Q. On what side of the stage was his usual position in the theatre?

A. On the back part of the stage, there was his particular place.

Q. On which side?

A. On the right-hand side of the stage.

Q. As you face it from the audience?

A. Yes, sir.

Q. That was the side of the President's box, was it, or was it not?

A. No, sir; the President's box was on the left-hand side.

Q. The left-hand side looking out from the stage?

A. Yes, sir.

Q. Mr. Spangler's place, you say, was on the other side?

A. Yes, next to the back door leading out to the alley.

Q. Where was your position?

A. Right on the flies, where we wind the curtain up, on the third story.

Q. Did you see Mr. Spangler that night after five o'clock?

A. Oh, yes; Mr. Spangler was there on the stage attending to his business, as usual.

Q. At what time did you see him?

A. In the early part of the night, I cannot tell exactly when; I never inquired to know the particular time. We had no time up there where we were. Only two men worked up there.

Q. How long did you see him before the President was shot?

A. I did not see Mr. Spangler at all before the President was shot. I myself was not thinking about anything like that going on. I was busy looking at the performance until I heard the report of a pistol.

Q. Did you not see Mr. Spangler during the play that night?

A. Yes, sir, he was there; he was on the stage during the play; he was obliged to be there.

Q. Did you see him in the first act?

A. Yes; he was there in the first act; I saw him then.

Q. Did you see him in the second act?

A. I do not remember seeing him in the second act.

Q. Were you down off the flies?

A. I was not off the flies. I could see him very well from the flies on the opposite side of the stage, next to the side where the President was sitting in his box. I could see

from my side over to that side of the stage.

Q. Were you on the side that the President's box was on?

A. No, I was on the other side.

Q. And Mr. Spangler's place was on the opposite side below?

A. Yes, sir.

Q. You say you did not see him during the second act?

A. I did not see him during the second act.

Q. Were you looking for him?

A. No, sir; I was not looking for him during the second act.

Q. Was he a sort of assistant stage manager?

A. Yes, sir; he was one of the regular stage managers, to shift the scenes at nights.

Q. From where you were could you see into the President's box?

A. I could. From where I was, I could see him plain.

A. And could you see also where Mr. Spangler was in the habit of being?

A. Yes, sir.

Q. Both of them were on the opposite side of the theatre from you?

A. Yes, sir, on the opposite side.

Q. Both of them, then, were on the same side with each other?

A. Yes, sir.

Q. What time in the first act did you see Spangler?

A. In the first act I saw him walking around the stage looking at the performance.

Q. Did he have his hat on?

A. Yes; he always had his hat on in the back entries.

Q. How was he dressed?

A. I cannot tell exactly what kind of clothes he had on, but just a common suit.

Q. Did he look as he does now?

A. Oh, no, sir; he did not look as he looks now.

Q. How was his face?

A. It is just as natural now as it was then.

Q. Did you ever see Mr. Spangler wear a moustache?

A. No, sir, I never did.

Q. From where you were up on the flies, you could sometimes see him where he was, and sometimes, when he would change his position, you would not see him?

A. I could not see him then.

Q. You just saw him occasionally, and his position generally was around on the side opposite to that where you were?

A. Yes, sir.

JOHN MILES, (Colored,)
a witness called for the prosecution, being duly sworn, testified as follows:

By the JUDGE ADVOCATE:

Q. Do you belong to Ford's Theatre; and have you been working there?

A. Yes, sir.

Q. Were you there on the night of the assassination of the President?

A. Yes, sir.

Q. Did you see J. Wilkes Booth there?

A. I saw him when he came there.

Q. What hour did he come? Tell us all you saw.

A. He came there, I think, between nine and ten o'clock, and he brought a horse from the stable and came to the back door and called "Ned Spangler" three times out of the theatre. Ned Spangler went across the stage to him. After that I did not see what became of Booth, and never noticed him any more until I heard a pistol go off. I then went up in sight of the President's box. The man up with me said some one had shot the President. The President had then gone out of sight. I could not see him. I went in a minute or two to the window and I heard the sound of horses' feet going out of the alley.

Q. Did you see anybody holding the horse out there?

A. I saw the boy holding the horse there; from the time I saw him he held him fifteen minutes.

Q. Was that after he called for Spangler?

A. Yes, sir.

Q. You mean Spangler, the prisoner here?

A. Yes, sir.

Q. You do not know what was said between them?

A. No, sir; I do not know anything about what was said between them. I did not understand a word. I only heard him called "Ned."

Q. You say he came up to the door with his horse between nine and ten o'clock. Do you know at what hour he put his horse in the little stable back of the theatre?

A. He had put his horse in the stable when I came over there. He and Ned Spangler and Jim Maddox came up from the stable in the evening, I think, about three o'clock. I judge it was about that time. I did not notice the time particularly. It was the time he came right through the theatre.

Q. How far is the little stable in which he kept the horse from the theatre?

A. Not more than fifty yards, if that.

Cross examined by Mr. EWING.

Q. Was the play going on when Booth rode up and called for Spangler?

A. They had just closed a scene and were getting ready to take off that scene at the time he called for Spangler. Spangler was at the second groove then, and pushed a scene across. Booth called him three times.

Q. Where were you then?

A. Up on the flies, about three and one-half stories from the stage.

Q. Was that in the third act?

A. I think it was in the third act.

Q. How long was it before the President was shot?

A. The President came in during the first act, and I think it was in the third act he was shot.

Q. About how long do you think it was from the time Booth came up there until the President was shot?

A. From the time he brought the horse there until the President was shot, I think it was about three-quarters of an hour. I saw Booth when he brought the horse from the stable to the door, and from that time until the President was shot, I think, was three-quarters of an hour.

Q. Do you know who held the horse?

A. John Peanuts held him; he was lying on a bench holding the horse when I noticed him. I was at the window pretty nearly all the time from the time Booth brought the horse until he went away. Every time I looked out of the window John Peanuts was lying on the bench holding the horse. I did not see any one else hold him.

Q. Was John Peanuts there when Booth came up?

A. I do not know; he was at the theatre, but I do not know whether he was at the door.

Q. Did you look out to see who was there?

A. There was nobody there when Booth came up, that I saw, because I was looking out of the window.

Q. Did Spangler go out?

A. He went to Booth. I supposed Booth was at the door.

Q. Spangler went to him?

A. He ran across the stage when Booth called him. Some person told him that Booth called him, and he ran across the stage to him.

Q. Do you know whether he went out of the door?

A. I do not know whether he did or not. I did not see him go out.

Q. Do you know how long Spangler stayed there?

A. No; because when I looked out again his boy was holding the horse.

Q. How long was that after he called Spangler?

A. Not more than ten or fifteen minutes.

Q. Do you know what Spangler had to do with Booth?

A. No, sir; only I saw him appear to be familiar with him, and keeping his company and so on when he was round about there.

Q. Did Booth treat him?

A. I do not know; I never saw him treat him.

Q. Did Spangler have anything to do with Booth's horses—hitch them up, or saddle them, or hold them?

A. Yes, sir; I have seen him hold them down at the stable.

Q. Did you know anything about his hitching Booth's horse or saddling him up?

A. I never saw him hitch any up there, but I have seen him hold the horse there at the stable door. John Peanuts always attended to the horses. I never saw Spangler put any gear on any of them.

Q. Do you know what place on the stage Spangler generally occupied?

A. He worked on the right-hand side, the side next to E street.

Q. The side the President's box was on?

A. Yes, sir; on that side.

Q. Could you see from where you were up in the flies?

A. I could see right straight down through the scenes on that side of the stage, and I always saw him work on that side.

Q. Was he on that side when Booth called him?

A. Yes, sir; he was.

Q. What was Spangler's business on that side? What kept him on that side?

A. He shoved the scenes at night on that side.

Q. Was there another man shoving from the other side?

A. Yes, sir; there was another man opposite to him.

Q. Did you see Spangler after you saw that Peanut John was holding Booth's horse?

A. I never saw him any more until I came down. I came down the stairs after the President was shot, and Spangler was out at the door.

Q. At what door?

A. At the same door Booth went out, when I came down stairs.

Q. Were there others out there?

A. Yes; there were some more men out there; I did not notice who they were, but some more besides him

Q. More men of the theatre?

A. That were at the theatre that night; there were some strangers out there then, I believe, because every person had got over the stage then that wanted to go over.

Q. How many men were out at the back door at that time?

A. Not more than two or three out of the door when I came down, because I came down in a very short time after I understood what it was, and Spangler came out and I asked him who it was that held the horse, and he told me "hush," "not to say nothing," and I did not say any more, though I knew who it was, because I saw the boy who was holding the horse. I knew that the person who brought the horse there rode him away again.

Q. You could not see Spangler all the time when he was on the stage, could you, from where you were?

A. When he was working on that side I could see him all the while if I looked for him.

Q. Did you look for him that night?

A. No; I did not notice him particularly that night more than usual. I would not have noticed him when I did, only I heard

Booth call him, and I noticed where he was when he went to Booth.

Q. He might have been on that side all night without your noticing it?

A. He might.

Q. You do not know, then, whether he was on that side or not?

A. He was on that side when I saw him before then, and he was on that side then.

Q But you did not look for him after that?

A. I did not look for him at all.

Q. What was it you asked Spangler when you came down?

A. I asked him who it was holding the horse at the door of the theatre.

Q. What did he say?

A. He told me to hush; not to say anything at all to him; and I never said no more to him.

Q. Was he excited?

A. He appeared to be.

Q. Was everybody excited?

A. Every person appeared to be very much excited.

Q. When you asked him who it was who was holding the horse, he said, "Hush; don't say anything to me?"

A. Yes, sir.

Q. And you say, "Hush; don't say anything to me?

A. I mean the same thing, to hush, not say anything about it. That was the word. Not thinking at the time, I said, "Do not say anything to me; but he said, "Dont say anything about it." That was the word; that was what he said, "Don't say anything about it."

Q. Do you know Spangler well?

A. Oh, yes; at least, I know him when I see him.

Q. Did you ever see him wear a moustache?

A. No, sir; I do not think I ever saw him wear a moustache.

By the JUDGE ADVOCATE:

Q. This remark he made to you, "Hush, don't say anything about it," was immediately after the killing of the President, was it?

A. Yes, sir; right at the door when I went out doors.

Q Did he make any other remark as a reason why you should not say anything about it?

A. No, sir; not a word to me.

Q. He made no other remark?

A. No, sir; not a word to me.

Q. Did you see Booth go out of the door?

A. No, sir; I did not see him go out of the door, but I heard his horse when it went out of the alley; whether it went right or left I cannot tell, but I heard the rapping of his feet on the ground.

Q. Was the door left open at that time when Booth was gone, or was it shut?

A. It was open when I came down stairs. I do not know whether it was left open from the time he came in and went out or not; but it was open when I got down stairs. I had to go down three and a-half stories before I got down on the stage, and when I got down it was open.

Q. Do you know anybody who probably heard your remark to Mr. Spangler and his reply to you?

.A. No, sir; I do not know any person that was noticing the words at all. There were a good many persons around, but I do not know that any of them was noticing the words used.

By the Court:

Q. When Booth called for Ned Spangler the first time, did you see where Spangler was?

A. Yes; when I noticed where Spangler was, he was right across the stage.

Q. You say Booth called him three times; when he called the first time, did you see where Spangler was?

A. I did not see where he was then, because I did not notice where he was until Booth called him the third time; then I saw where he was standing.

Q. Where did Spangler meet Booth then?

A. He went towards the door. After he got underneath the flies, I could not see him any more.

Q. Then you lost sight of him as he was going to the door?

A. Yes sir; as he went across the stage.

Q. How long was he with him? Can you tell?

A. I cannot tell, because I did not see Spangler again until I came down from off the flies.

Q. When Spangler told you to hush, not to say anything about it, was he near the door?

A. He was, I suppose, about a yard and a half from the door.

Q. Was anybody else near the door but him?

A. There was nobody else near the door that I could see; that is, there was nobody else between him and me and the door.

Q. Did he have hold of the door at that time?

A. No; he was walking across the door when I spoke to him; he was walking across the door, in front of the door, outside the door. There was nobody else between him and me and the door, because I brushed right up to him and asked who was holding the horse.

Q. Right at the door was it light or dark?

A. Dark right at that door; and it was a dark night anyhow.

Q. But there was no light right there?

A. No light there.

By Mr. Ewing:

Q. Were you and Spangler inside the door or outside the door?

A. Outside.

Q. Where were the other people that you say were about there?

A. They were standing just round about there, some of them a little further from the door.

Q. Still further outside the door?

A. Yes, further outside the door.

Q. You were between these people and the door?

A. Yes, sir.

Q. And all were in the alley?

A. Yes, sir.

By the Court:

Q. Did he appear to be covering that door?

A. No, sir; he did not appear to be covering it at all.

Q. Did he act as if he was trying to prevent persons from getting in or out that door?

A. No. He did appear to be excited. That was the only thing I discovered about him—very much excited.

Q. At that time Booth had gone out of the alley?

A. Yes, sir; he had gone out of the alley.

JOHN F. SLEICKMANN,

a witness called for the prosecution, being duly sworn, testified as follows:

By the JUDGE ADVOCATE:

Q. Have you been connected with Ford's Theatre in this city?

A. Yes, sir.

Q. Were you there on the night of the assassination of the President?

A. I was.

Q. Do you know J. Wilkes Booth?

A. Yes, sir.

Q. Did you, or not, see him on that night, and if so, at what hour and under what circumstances?

A. I saw him about nine o'clock, I guess it was. He came up on a horse and came in a little back door to the theatre. Ned Spangler was standing there by one of the wings, and Booth said to him, "Ned, you will help me all you can, won't you? and Ned said, "Oh, yes."

Q. I understand you to say that as Booth came up to the door with his horse, he said that?

A. When he came in the door after he got off the horse.

Q. Was that his salutation, the way he first addressed Spangler? Were those the first words he spoke?

A. Yes, sir; the first words that I heard.

Q. "Ned, you will help me all you can, won't you?"

A. Yes, sir; and Ned said, "Oh, yes."

Q How long was that before the President was shot?

A. I should judge it to be about an hour and a half.

Q. Did you observe the horse afterwards, by whom it was held?

A. I did not.

Q. You did not see Booth any more?

A. I just got a glimpse of him as he was going out the first entrance on the right hand side.

Q. What hour was that when you saw him going out of the first entrance?

A. About half-past ten o'clock, I think. That was after he shot the President.

Q. You mean, he went out the back door?

A. I do not know where he went after that. I did not see him.

Q. You say you saw him going out?

A. I saw him going out the entrance near the prompter's place.

Q. That is near the back door?

A. Yes; you go there, and turn to your right, to go out the door.

Cross-examined by Mr. EWING:

Q. Did you hear Booth calling for Spangler?

A. No, sir. He just came up and said, "Ned, you will help me all you can, won't you?" and Ned said, "Oh, yes."

Q. Where were they then?

A. Right by the back door.

Q. Did Booth ride up?

A. I guess so. I did not see him on the horse; but the horse was standing there when he came in the back door.

Q. Was anybody holding the horse then?

A. I did not see anybody holding the horse at all.

Q. Was not Spangler holding him?

A. No; Booth was talking to Ned.

Q. Was Booth holding the horse?

A. No; Booth had come inside the door.

Q. Did you see the horse?

A. I saw the horse; he left the door open.

Q. But you cannot say whether anybody was holding the horse or not?

A. I cannot. It was dark out there, and I could not tell much about it.

Q. What was your place in the theatre?

A. I was assistant property-man.

Q. What was your position on the stage; any particular place?

A. We have to set the furniture and everything of that kind on the stage.

Q. What was Spangler's position on the stage?

A. Stage carpenter; shoving the scenes, and so on.

Q. Is he the principal stage carpenter?

A. No, sir, Mr. Gifford is the principal stage carpenter.

Q. Spangler is just a rough carpenter?

A. He was helping Mr. Gifford there; hired by Mr. Gifford.

Q. What was Spangler's place on the stage during a play?

A. He had to shove the scenes together.

Q. On which side?

A. I do not know on which side particularly.

Q. Were you about that night?

A. Yes, sir.

Q. Were you on the stage?

A. I was.

Q During the whole play?

A. I had to go down to the apothecary store to get a few little articles to use in the piece; I do not believe I was out more than that, except when I went into the restaurant next door.

JOSEPH BURROUGH,

a witness called for the prosecution, being duly sworn, testified as follows:

By the JUDGE ADVOCATE:

Q. State whether or not you have been connected with Ford's Theatre in this city?

A. Yes, sir, I have been.

Q. In what capacity?

A. I used to stand at the stage door, and then carry bills in the daytime; and I used to attend Booth's horse, see that he was fed and cleaned.

Q. Did you know John Wilkes Booth in his lifetime?

A. I knew him while he kept his horse there in that stable.

Q. Do you speak of the stable immediately back of the theatre?

A. Yes, sir.

Q. Did you see him on the afternoon of the 14th of April?

A. I saw him when he brought his horse to the stable, between five and six o'clock.

Q. State what he did?

A. He brought the horse and hallooed out for Spangler.

Q. Did Spangler go down to the stable?

A. Yes, sir; he went out there. Mr. Booth asked him for a halter; he had none there; and he sent Jake after one up stairs.

Q. How long did they remain together then?

A. I do not know. Jim Maddox was down there then, too.

Q. Did you see him again at a later hour that evening?

A. I saw him on the stage that night.

Q. Did you, or not, see him when he came with his horse between nine and ten o'clock that night.

A. No sir, I did not see him when he came up the alley with his horse.

Q. Did you see the horse at the door?

A. I saw him when Spangler called me out there to hold the horse.

Q. State all that happened at that time what was said and done.

A. I can not.

Q. Why? Do you not recollect it?

A. No, sir.

Q. Did you see Booth when he came there with his horse?

A. No, sir, I did not see him.

Q. Did you hear him call for Ned Spangler?

A. No, sir, I heard Debonay calling Ned, that Booth wanted him.

Q. Who held Booth's horse that evening?

A. Nobody but me; I held him that night.

Q. Who gave you the horse to hold?

A. Spangler.

Q. At what hour?

A. I cannot tell exactly what hour; between nine and ten I think.

Q. How long was it before the President was shot?

A. I held the horse about fifteen minutes.

Q. What did Spangler say when he asked you to hold the horse?

A. He just told me to hold it. I said I could not, I had to go in and attend to my door. He told me to hold the horse, and if there was anything to lay the blame on him. So I held the horse.

Q. Did you hold him near the door?

A. No; I was sitting over against the house there, on a carpenter's bench.

Q. Did you hear the report of the pistol?

A. Yes, sir.

Q. Were you still on the bench when Booth came out?

A. I had got off the bench then.

Q. What did he say when he came out?

A. He told me to give him his horse.

Q. Had you got up to the door?

A. No; I was still out by the bench.

Q. Did he do anything besides that?

A. He knocked me down.

Q. With his hand or not?

A. He struck me with the butt of a knife.

Q. Did he do that as he mounted his horse?

A. Yes, sir, he had one foot in the stirrup.

Q. Did he also strike or kick you?

A. He kicked me.

Q. As he got on the horse?

A. Yes, sir.

Q. Did he say nothing while getting on the horse?

A. He said nothing else; he only hallooed to me to give him his horse.

Q. Did he ride off immediately?

A. Yes, sir.

Q. State whether or not you were in the President's box that afternoon.

A. Yes, sir; I was up there.

Q. Who decorated or fixed the box for the President?

A. Harry Ford put the flags around it.

Q. Was or was not the prisoner Spangler with you in the box?

A. He was up there with me. I went after him to take out the partition.

Q. What was he doing?

A. Harry Ford told me to go in with Spangler and take out the partition of the box, as the President and General Grant were coming there. I then went after Spangler.

Q. Do you remember whether, while Spangler was doing that, he said anything in regard to the President?

A. He made remarks and laughed.

Q. What were they?

A. He said, "Damn the President and General Grant."

Q. While damning the President, or after damning him, did he say anything else?

A. I said to him, "What are you damning the man for—a man that has never done harm to you?" He said he ought to be cursed when he got so many men killed.

Q. Did he, or not, say anything in regard to what he wished in that connection?

A. I do not remember that.

Q. Did he or did he not say what he wished might happen to Gen. Grant?

Mr. Ewing objected to the question.

A. I do not remember that.

Q. Was or was there not anything said, in the course of that conversation, as to what might or might not be done to the President or Gen. Grant?

Mr. Ewing objected to the question.

A. No, sir; I did not hear anything.

Cross-examined by Mr. Ewing:

Q. You say you did not hear anybody calling out for Spangler?

A. I heard Debonay call for him, and he told him Mr. Booth wanted him out in the alley.

Q. Who is Debonay?

A. He used to be a kind of actor there.

Q. Debonay called him, and told him Booth wanted him?

A. Yes, sir.

Q. How long was it after that that Spangler called you?

A. I do not know how long; not very long; about six or seven or eight minutes.

Q. What were you doing when Spangler called you?

A. I was sitting at the first entrance on the left.

Q. What business were you doing?

A. I was attending to the stage-door there.

Q. What had you to do at the stage-door there?

A. I keep strangers out, and prevent those coming in who do not belong there.

Q. You told him that you could not hold the horse; that you had to attend that door?

A. Yes, sir.

Q. And he said what?

A. If there was anything wrong to blame it on him.

Q. Were you around in front of the theatre that night?

A. I was out there while the curtain was down. I go out between every act, while the curtain is down, when the curtain is up I go inside.

Q. Did you see Booth in front of the theatre?

A. No, sir, I did not.

Q. Did you see Spangler in front of the theatre?

A. No, sir.

Q. Did you ever see Spangler wear a moustache?

A. No, sir.

Q. Do you know whether Spangler wore any whiskers of any kind that night?

A. I did not see him wear any.

Q. Was not Spangler in the habit of hitching up Booth's horse?

A. He wanted to take the bridle off, and Booth would not let him.

Q. When was that?

A. Between five and six that evening. At first he wanted to take the saddle off, but Booth would not let him; then he wanted to take the bridle off, but he would not agree to it, and he just put a halter around the horse's neck. He took the saddle off afterwards, though.

Q. Was not Spangler in the habit of bridling and saddling, and hitching up Booth's horse?

A. When I was not there he used to hitch him up.

Q. Was he not in the habit of holding him, too, when you were not about?

A. Yes, sir; and he used to feed him when I was not about.

Q. Then you and Spangler together attended to Booth's horse?

A. Sometimes. Mr. Gifford gave me the job to attend to. He asked me if I knew anything about horses, and I told him I knew a little about them. Then he asked me if I would not attend to Booth's horse, and he gave me the job.

Q. And Spangler used to help you about it?

A. Yes, sir.

Q. And when you were not there Spangler did it himself?

A. Yes, sir; and Spangler used to go after feed sometimes.

Q. Do you know the way Booth went out after he jumped out of the President's box?

A. No, sir; I was not in the alley.

Q. Do you know the passage between the green room and the scenes, through which Booth ran, which leads right out to the door?

A. Yes, sir; that is on the other side of the stage.

Q. The one that Booth ran through when he went out into the alley?

A. I do not know what entrance he ran through.

Q. Was Booth about the theatre a great deal?

A. He was not about there much; he used to go there sometimes.

Q. Which way would he enter the theatre generally?

A. On Tenth street.

Q. Did he sometimes enter back?

A. Sometimes.

Q. How far was the stable where Booth kept his horse from the back entrance of the theatre?

A. About two hundred yards.

Q. Do you recollect what act was being played when you first went out to hold Booth's horse?

A. I think it was the first scene of the third act. The scene had curtains on the door.

Q. Was that scene being played when you went out to hold the horse?

A. Yes, sir; they had just been closing in.

By the JUDGE ADVOCATE:

Q. You have the nickname of "Peanuts" about there?

A. Yes, sir; I used to stay at a stand in front of the theatre, and they call me "John Peanuts" about there.

Q. Was there more than one horse in the stable that evening?

A. Only one—that is all I saw—and Booth brought that there.

Q. Do I understand you to say that there was only one horse in the stable that afternoon?

A. That was all I saw when I was there, between five and six.

Q. You were not in the stable afterwards?

A. No.

By Mr. EWING:

Q. Do you know on what side of the theatre Spangler worked?

A. Always on the left side.

Q. Is that the side the President's box was on?

A. Yes, sir.

Q. Was that the side you attended the door on?

A. Yes, sir.

Q. When you were away, did he not attend the door for you?

A. Yes, sir, when I was away, he used to attend the door.

Q. His position, then, was near to where your position was?

A. Yes, sir.

Q. What door was that; the door that went into the little alley?

A. Yes, sir, from Tenth street.

Q. You attended there to see that nobody came in that was not authorized to come?

A. Yes, sir; when the curtain was down, I used to go outside and stay until the curtain was up.

Q. When the play was going on, who was there on that side to shove the scenes except Spangler? Anybody?

A. There was another man there on that side; two men worked on this side, and three on the other.

Q. Who was the man that worked with Spangler on that side?

A. I think his name is Simmons.

Q. Who are the men that worked on the other side?

A. One of them is Skeggy, another is Jake, and I do not know the other fellow's name.

Q. While the play was going on, did these men always stay there?

A. Yes, sir, they are always about there.

Q. They had to stay there in order to shove the scenes, had they not?

A. Yes, they always have to be there when the whistle blows, and shove them.

Q. Did they usually stay there on their sides?

A. Yes, sir; but sometimes, when a scene would stand a whole act, they would go around on the other side, and those on the other side would come on their side.

Q. But did not go out?

A. Sometimes they used to go out—not very often, though.

By the JUDGE ADVOCATE:

Q. Was there another horse in that stable some days before, or not?

A. Yes, there was one other horse there—two horses there one day.

Q How long before?

A. Booth brought a horse and buggy there. I cannot tell you when it was.

Q. Do you remember the color or appearance of the horse?

A. It was a little horse; I do not remember the color.

Q. Do you remember whether he was blind of one eye?

A. No, sir. The fellow that brought the horse there used to go with Booth very often.

Q. Do you see among the prisoners here the man who brought the horse?

A. No, sir; I do not see him there, [pointing to the dock of the prisoners.] It was the fellow who lived at the Navy Yard, I think. I saw him going in a house down there one day, when I was carrying bills there. I do not know whether he lived there or not.

Q. Do you remember his name?

A. No, sir; I never heard his name.

By the COURT:

Q. Did you see Booth at the instant he left the back door of the theatre after the assassination of the President?

A. He rode off.

Q Did you see him when he came out of the door?

A. Yes, sir.

Q. What door did he come out of, the small one or the large one?

A. The small one.

Q. Was there anybody else at that door?

A. No, sir, I did not see anybody else.

Q. Did Spangler pass through that door leading into the passage at any time while you were sitting at the door—the passage toward the street?

A. I did not take notice.

Q. You did not see him go out or come in while you were there?

A. No, sir.

Q. You said that you were in the President's box on the day of the murder?

A. Yes, sir.

Q. What time in the day was that?

A. About three o'clock.

Q. Did all the employees in the theatre know that the President was to be there that night?

A. I heard Harry Ford say so.

Q. Anybody else? Did you hear Spangler speak of it?

A. No; I told him the President was coming there.

Q. What time did you say you were there?

A. It was about three o'clock when we went up to take out the partition.

Q. Who were in the box at the time the partition was taken out?

A. Spangler, Jake, and myself.

Q. Who is Jake?

A. All I know is that his name is Jake.

Q. A black man or a white man?

A. A white man.

Q. Employed there?

A. Yes, he used to be a stage-carpenter there.

Q Was he regularly employed in that theatre at that time?

A. He worked there day and night.

Q. Had he been working there for some time?

A. He had been working there about three weeks.

Q. When they were there, how long did they stay in the box?

A. I stayed there until they took the partition out, and sat down in the box.

Q. Did you observe what else they did in the box?

A. No, sir. Spangler said it would be a nice place to sleep in after the partition was down. That is all I recollect.

MRS. MARY ANN TURNER,

a witness called for the prosecution, being duly sworn, testified as follows:

By the JUDGE ADVOCATE:

Q. State to the Court where you reside in this city.

A. I reside in the rear of Ford's Theatre.

Q. How far from it?

A. As far as from here to where that gentleman sits over there, or may be a little farther, [pointing to one of the counsel for the accused, a distance of about eight feet.]

Q. Did you know John Wilkes Booth?

A. I knew him when I saw him.

Q. Will you state what you saw of him on the afternoon of the 14th of April last?

A. That afternoon I saw him, I think, to the best of my recollection, between three and four o'clock, standing in the back door of Ford's Theatre with a lady by his side. I did not take any particular notice of him at that time, but I turned from the door, and I saw no more of him until, to the best of my recollection, between seven and eight or near about eight o'clock that night, when he brought a horse up to the back door, and

opened the door and called for a man by the name of 'Ned' three times—to the best of my recollection, not more than three times. This "Ned" came to him, and I heard him say to "Ned" in a low voice, "tell Maddox to come here." I then saw Maddox come. He [Booth] said something in a very low voice to this Maddox, and I saw Maddox reach out his hand and take the horse, but where "Ned" went I cannot tell. This Booth went on into the theatre.

Q. Did you see him or hear him when he came out after the assassination of the President?

A. I only heard the horse going very rapidly out of the alley, and I ran immediately to my door and opened it, but he was gone; I did not see him at all.

Q. Did you see the man named "Ned," of whom you speak?

A. Yes, sir.

Q. At what time did you see him?

A. I rushed to the door immediately, the crowd came out, and this time this man "Ned" came out of the theatre.

Q. Which of those men in the dock is it?

A. There he sits with dark shirt and dark coat on, [pointing to the accused, Edward Spangler.]

Q. Spangler, you mean?

A. Yes, sir, Ned Spangler; and said I to him, "Mr. Ned, you know that man Booth called you?" Said he, "No, I know nothing about it," and then he went down the alley.

Q. Was that all that occurred between you and him?

A. That was all that was said between me and him.

Cross-examined by Mr. Ewing:

Q. How far is your house from the back door of the theatre?

A. My front door fronts to the back of the theatre. It comes out into the open alley, which leads up to the door. There is another house between mine and the theatre. The two houses are adjoining, and my house stands as far from the door of the theatre as from here to the post. [About twenty-two feet.] I think it would allow that space for the two houses.

Q. Did you see where Spangler went after he called Maddox?

A. No, sir, I did not see where Spangler went after he called Maddox.

Q. Did he go off?

A. I do not remember whether he went off or not. I did not see him any more.

Q. Did you see him go in to call Maddox?

A. Yes, sir; he turned from the door to call Maddox.

Q. Did you hear him call him?

A. No, sir, I did not hear him call Maddox.

Q. Did you see Spangler come out again?

A. I do not remember whether he came out or not; I do not think I did see him come out.

MRS. MARY JANE ANDERSON,

a witness called for the prosecution, being duly sworn, testified as follows:

By the JUDGE ADVOCATE:

Q. Will you state where you live in this city?

A. I live between E and F and Ninth and Tenth streets.

Q. Do you live near Ford's Theatre?

A. Yes, sir, right back of the theatre.

Q. Does your house adjoin that of Mrs. Turner, who has just testified?

A. Yes, sir, my house and hers are adjoining.

Q. Did you know John Wilkes Booth?

A. Yes, sir, I knew him by sight.

Q. Did you see him on the afternoon or night of the 14th of April last?

A. Yes, sir, I saw him in the morning.

Q. State what you saw?

A. I saw him down there by the stable, and he went out of the alley, and I did not see him again until between two and three o'clock in the afternoon, when I saw him standing in the back theatre door, in the alley that leads out back. He and a lady were standing together talking. I stood in my gate, and I looked right wishful at him. He and this lady were pointing up and down the alley, as if they were talking in their conversation about the alley, as it seemed to me; and they stood there a considerable while. After that, they both turned into the theatre together. I never saw him any more until at night. I went up stairs pretty early, and when I went up stairs, there was a carriage drove up the alley, and after that I heard a horse step down the alley again. I looked out of the window, and it seemed as if the gentleman was leading this horse down the alley. He did not get any further than the end of the alley, and in a few minutes he returned back again. I still looked out to see who it was. He came up to the theatre door, this gentleman did, with the horse by the bridle. He pushed the door open, and said something in a low tone, and then in a loud voice he called, "Ned," four times. There was a colored man up at the window, and he said, "Mr. Ned, Mr. Booth calls you." That is the way I came to know it was Mr. Booth. It was dark, and I could not see his face. When Mr. Ned came, Booth said to him, in a low tone, "Tell Maddox to come here." Then Mr. Ned went back and Maddox came out. They said something to each other, but I could not understand from my window what the words were. After that Mr. Maddox took hold of this horse. It seems it was between him and Mr. Ned. He had this horse. He carried it from before my door, right at the corner of my house, around to where the work-bench was; that stood at the right side of the house. I could not see the horse, but they both returned back into the

theatre again. This man that carried the horse up went in the door, too. The horse stood out there a considerable while. It kept up a great deal of stamping on the stones, and I said, "I wonder what is the matter with that horse;" it kept stamping so. After a while I saw this person have a hold of the horse, and he kept the horse walking backwards and forwards. I suppose the horse was there completely an hour and a half altogether; then I saw the door open; I did not see any person passing backwards and forwards, and in about ten minutes after that I saw this man [Booth] come out of the door with something in his hand glittering. I did not know what it was; but still I thought some person ran out of the theatre and jumped on the horse. He had come out of the theatre door so quick, that it seemed like as if he but touched that horse, and it was gone like a flash of lightning. I thought to myself "that horse must surely have run off with that gentleman." Presently I saw a rush out of that door, and heard the people saying, "Which way did he go?" and "which way did he go?" and still I did not know what was the matter. I asked a gentleman what was the matter, and he said the President was shot. "Why," said I, "who shot him?" Said he, "That man who went out on the horse; did you see him?" I said I saw him when he first came out. That was the last time I saw him to know him.

Q. Did you see the prisoner Spangler at that time?

A. Yes, sir. I saw Mr. Spangler after that. After that I came down stairs, and was at the door talking. I went up to the theatre door, and I saw Mr. Spangler when he came out of the door. Some one said, "Did you see that man?" I said to Mr. Spangler, "Mr. Spangler, that gentleman called you." Said he, "No, be did not." Said I, "Yes, he did; he called you." He said, "No, he did not; he did not call me." I said, "He did call you," and I kept on saying so. With that, he walked down toward the alley, and I did not see him any more until Sunday; but I did not say anything to him at all then. I had no other conversation with him.

Cross-examined by Mr. EWING:

Q. Did you know Mr. Maddox?

A. Yes, sir.

Q. What kind of a looking man is he?

A. He has a kind of a reddish skin, and sometimes a kind of palish and light hair.

Q. How old a man is he?

A. I suppose he is about 25 or 26.

Q. Have you seen him often?

A. Yes, sir; I have seen him very often. I live close by there. I used to work for him right smart. I used to wash some pieces for him, and used to go there to the door and bring them. I know him very well by sight.

Q. Was it he who held this horse during all the time it was in the alley there?

A. No, sir; it did not seem like as if he held it all the time; but he took hold of the horse, and it seemed as if he had him a little while, and he moved him out of my sight; and then I saw him return and go into the theatre. This gentleman had on a light coat.

Q. Then who held the horse when he went in the theatre?

A. I did not see because it was carried around from my door, and I could not see it out of my window. It was carried around the house like, out of sight; but then when it was in a commotion, it seemed as if there was a man had it, but I could not tell who he was.

Q. When the horse was moving up and down, it seemed as if a man had it?

A. Yes; as if a man was keeping it in motion all the time.

Q. Marching it up and down to keep it from fretting and stamping?

A. Yes, sir; it was making a great deal of noise, stamping its feet; and it seemed as if a man was carrying it backward and forward all the time.

Q. Mr. Spangler just came to the door, and Booth said to him, "Tell Mr. Maddox to come out?"

A. Yes, sir.

Q. And then Spangler went in, did he?

A. Yes, sir, he went in; and then it seemed as if he came out again.

Q. Are you sure he came out again?

A. It seems to me like as if he came out again. Whether he came out or not I am not certain; but I know he came to the door when Mr. Booth called.

Q. But you are not certain that he came out again?

A. No, sir; I am not certain whether he came out again or no; but I know he came out to the door when Booth called him, and he told him to tell Maddox to come out, and Maddox came out to this Mr. Booth, and had some conversation with him; but I could not hear what it was.

Q. How long was it from the time that Booth rode up there until the people said he had shot the President?

A. I suppose it was about an hour—not quite an hour—from the time he came up there to the time they said the President was shot. I think it was almost an hour; but I do not think it was quite an hour.

Q. Did you see the man who held the horse at the time Booth ran out and rode away on him?

A. Yes, sir, I saw the man, but I could not tell who the man was. I know a man had hold of the horse when Booth came out, because, when he came out, he was walking the horse up and down, and it seemed as if the minute he touched the horse the horse was gone. I was looking down the alley to see which way he went, and when I looked back again I did not see anybody.

Q. Did that man look like Mr. Maddox?

A. He looked very much like Mr. Maddox to me. I know Mr. Maddox. He wears a light coat, and this man seemed as if he had a light coat on. It was pretty dark there that night; I could not see distinctly from my window, but the coat he had on seemed as if it was light.

Q. How far was he from you when you say you thought it was Mr. Maddox?

A. He was right near the door.

Q. How far from where you were?

A. About as far as from here to that window, or a little further, [about fifteen feet.]

Q. Whereabouts was the horse just at the time when Booth ran out the door?

A. Standing right at the door.

Q. And this man with the light coat on was standing right by him?

A. I cannot say whether he was standing by him, because I was looking at the man when he rushed out the door so, and everything was in such a twinkling of an eye that I could not say distinctly it was the man with the light coat on; but I know there was a man holding the horse all the time as far as I could see.

Q. It was not Mr. Spangler that was holding him?

A. I do not know. It seems to me it was between all three of them. They all three seemed to be out there with the horse, apparently. I knew Mr. Ned came out to the door, and then Mr. Maddox came out, and then it seemed as if Mr. Ned came out again.

Q. But you are not certain that he did come out again?

A. No, sir, I am not very certain of that, but I know there were three men in it altogether.

Q. That is, three men connected with it in some way?

A. Yes, sir; three men connected with it in some way.

Q. But you cannot say that you saw Mr. Spangler, except when he came out of the door and Booth told him to call Maddox.

A. No, sir; I cannot say for certain; but I know one of the men had on a light coat.

Q. That was the one that was holding the horse?

A. Yes, sir.

MAJOR HENRY R. RATHBONE,

a witness called for the prosecution, being duly sworn, testified as follows:

By the JUDGE ADVOCATE:

Q. Will you state to the Court whether or not you were in the box of the President on the night of his assassination at Ford's Theatre?

A. I was.

Q. State all the circumstances that came under your observation in connection with that crime.

A. On the evening of the 14th of April last, at about twenty minutes past eight o'clock, I, in company with Miss Harris, left my residence at the corner of Fifteenth and H streets, and joined the President and Mrs. Lincoln, and went with them, in their carriage, to Ford's Theatre in Tenth street. On reaching the theatre, when the presence of the President became known, the actors stopped playing, the band struck up "Hail to the Chief," the audience rose and received him with vociferous cheering. The party proceeded along in the rear of the dress-circle, and entered the box that had been set apart for their reception. On entering the box, there was a large arm chair that was placed nearest the audience, furthest from the stage, which the President took and occupied during the whole of the evening, with one exception, when he got up and put on his coat, and returned and sat down again. When the second scene of the third act was being performed, and while I was intently observing the proceedings upon the stage, with my back towards the door, I heard the discharge of a pistol behind me, and, looking around, saw, through the smoke, a man between the door and the President. At the same time, I heard him shout some word which I thought was "Freedom!" I instantly sprang towards him and seized him. He wrested himself from my grasp, and made a violent thrust at my breast with a large knife. I parried the blow by striking it up, and received a wound several inches deep in my left arm, between the elbow and the shoulder. The orifice of the wound was about an inch and a half in length, and extended upwards towards the shoulder several inches. The man rushed to the front of the box, and I endeavored to seize him again, but only caught his clothes as he was leaping over the railing of the box. The clothes, as I believe, were torn in the attempt to seize him. As he went over upon the stage, I cried out with a loud voice, "Stop that man." I then turned to the President. His position was not changed; his head was slightly bent forward, and his eyes were closed. I saw that he was unconscious, and supposing him mortally wounded, rushed to the door for the purpose of calling medical aid. On reaching the outer door of the passage-way I found it barred by a heavy piece of plank, one end of which was secured in the wall, and the other resting against the door. It had been so securely fastened that it required considerable force to remove it. This wedge or bar was about four feet from the floor. Persons up on the outside were beating against the door for the purpose of entering. I removed the bar and the door was opened. Several persons, who represented themselves as surgeons, were allowed to enter. I saw there Col. Crawford, and requested him to prevent other persons from entering the box; I then returned

to the box, and found the surgeons examining the President's person. They had not yet discovered the wound. As soon as it was discovered, it was determined to remove him from the theatre. He was carried out, and I then proceeded to assist Mrs. Lincoln, who was intensely excited, to leave the theatre. On reaching the head of the stairs I requested Major Potter to aid me in assisting Mrs. Lincoln across the street to the house where the President was being conveyed. The wound which I had received had been bleeding very profusely, and on reaching the house, feeling very faint from the loss of blood, I seated myself in the hall, and soon after fainted away, and was laid upon the floor. Upon the return of consciousness I was taken to my residence. In a review of the transactions, it is my confident belief that the time which elapsed between the discharge of the pistol and the time when the assassin leaped from the box did not exceed 30 seconds. Neither Mrs. Lincoln nor Miss Harris had left their seats.

Q. You did not know Booth yourself, did you?

A. No, sir.

Q. Do you think you would recognize him from a photograph?

A. I should be unable to do so as being the man in that box. I myself have seen him on the stage some time since.

By the Court:

Q. What distance was the assassin from the President when you first saw him after hearing the report?

A. The distance from the door to where the President was sitting, to the best of my recollection, was about four or five feet, and this man was standing between the door and the President.

By the Judge Advocate:

Q. Will you look at that knife [exhibiting a knife to the witness] and say if it appears to you to be such a one as he used? I believe the blood is still on the blade.

A. I think this knife might have made a wound similar to the one I received. I could not recognize the knife. I merely saw the gleam.

[The knife was offered in evidence without objection, and is marked Exhibit No. 28.]

Q. Did you notice how the blade was held in the hand of the assassin when he held it?

A. The blade was held in a horizontal position, I should think, and the nature of the wound would indicate it. It came with a sweeping blow down from above.

MAY 19.

John Greenawalt,

a witness called for the prosecution, being duly sworn, testified as follows:

By the Judge Advocate:

Q. Will you state whether or not you are the keeper of the Pennsylvania House in this city?

A. I am.

Q. Where is that house situated?

A. At Nos. 357 and 359 C street, between Four-and-a-half and Sixth streets.

Q. Are you acquainted with the prisoner Atzerodt?

A. I am.

Q. Were you or not acquainted with J. Wilkes Booth in his lifetime?

A. I was never acquainted with him.

Q. Did you know him by sight?

A. I never knew him. A man came to the house; from the description I had of him afterwards it was Booth. He has been there to see Atzerodt.

Q. Did you see him?

A. I did.

Q. Look at that photograph and see if you recognize it as the photograph of that man? [Exhibit No. 1.]

A. That is the person.

Q. State whether or not that person, Booth, had frequent interviews with the prisoner Atzerodt at the Pennsylvania House.

A. He had.

Q. What was the character of those interviews?

A. Atzerodt generally sat in the sitting-room, and Booth would come in through the hall. Sometimes he would not enter the room at all; he would walk in and walk back. Atzerodt would get up and follow him out. They frequently had interviews in front of my house. Several times that I walked on the steps they walked off down by the livery stable, towards the National Hotel, and stood and held interviews there.

Q. Did you or not at any time hear the prisoner Atzerodt speak of expecting to have plenty of gold soon? State what he said on that subject.

A. Once, he and some more—there was a number of young men from Port Tobacco met him there, and they had been drinking. He asked me to take a drink. I took a drink, and he said, "Greenawalt, I am pretty near broke, but I have always got friends enough to give me as much money as will see me through; though," said he, "I am going away some of these days, but I will return with as much gold as will keep me all my life-time."

Q. When was it that he made that declaration?

A. It must have been nine or ten days after he first came to my house.

Q. What month was that?

A. He came there on the 18th of March last, I believe. I think it must have been about the 30th or 31st of March or the 1st of April when this happened, as near as I can remember.

Q. Was he or not in the habit when in the city, of stopping at your house?

A. He stopped there before this last time. He stopped over night; he never stopped any length of time.

Q. Will you state how long before the assassination he left your house?

A. I think on Wednesday morning.

Q. Had he any baggage with him?

A. No, sir.

Q. Will you state when you next saw him again?

A. I saw him next on Saturday morning, between two and three o'clock, after the assassination.

Q Did he come to your home and ask for a room at that hour?

A. I had just come in the house myself and went to my room. About five minutes afterwards a servant came up with a five dollar bill and told me. "there is a man come in with Atzerodt who wants lodgings and wants to pay for it." So I went down and gave the man his change. I had an uneasiness about the thing myself—thought there was something wrong.

Q. Did they take a room together?

A. Yes, sir. Atzerodt asked for his old room, and I told him it was occupied. I told him he would have to go with this gentleman. So I gave the man his change—this Thomas—and told the servant to show him to his room, and Atzerodt was going to follow him. Said I, "Atzerodt you have not registered." Said he, "Do you want my name?" Said I, "Certainly." He hesitated some, but stepped back and registered, and went to his room. That was the last I saw of him.

Q. Will you describe the appearance of that man who was with him?

A. He was a man about five feet seven or eight inches high, and his weight was about one hundred and forty pounds, I should judge.

Q. How was he dressed?

A. Poorly dressed, and in dark. His pants were worn through at the back near the heels. I took notice of that as he walked out of the door to go to his room. He was quite dark complexioned and very much weather-beaten. He had dark hair.

Q. Had he the appearance of a laboring man?

A. Yes, sir; the appearance of a laboring man.

Q. Could you express an opinion as to whether the clothes in which he was dressed were such as he would probably ordinarily wear, or were assumed as a disguise? Have you an opinion on that subject?

A. I judged them to be more of a disguise. I think it was a broadcloth coat he had on, very much worn, though.

Q. The whole appearance, you say, was shabby?

A. Yes, sir.

Q. What name did he assume?

A. Sam. Thomas.

Q. What became of that man the next morning?

A. He got up about five o'clock I think, and left the house. That was what the servant told me. There was a lady stopping there, and I had given the servant orders to get her a carriage to take her to the railroad depot for the 6.15 train. She had left before I got up, and as the servant was going out of the door, this man Thomas went out and asked the way to the railway depot.

Q. He had no baggage?

A. No, sir; not any.

Q. He came between two and three, you say, and left at five?

A. Yes, sir.

Q. Did Atzerodt remain?

A. Atzerodt left shortly afterwards, and he walked towards Sixth street. As the servant came back from getting the carriage he met Atzerodt and said to him. "Atzerodt, what brings you out so early this morning?" "Well," said he, "I have got business." These were all the words.

Q. In what direction was he going?

A. Towards Sixth street—that is, west from my house.

Q. Had he paid his bill?

A. No. sir.

Q. He left without paying?

A. Yes. sir.

Q. When did you see him again?

A. I have not seen him since.

Q. Do you recognize him among these prisoners?

A. Yes, sir; there he sits. [Pointing to George A. Atzerodt.]

Q. Is this the first time you have seen him since?

A. It is.

Q. What was the manner of these men that night? Did you observe anything unusual, any excitement about them?

A. No, sir. There was no excitement about them. This man Thomas stared at me. He kept a close eye on me as I came in.

Q. Did they have any conversation with each other in your presence?

A. No, sir.

Q. Which of them asked for the room?

A. Thomas asked for it.

Q. Did he ask for both? How did they happen to have the same room?

A. He just asked for himself. Atzerodt was lying on the settee in the corner of the room as I came in, and Thomas was standing at the counter, at the register.

Q. How did it happen, then, that they went to the same room?

A. Atzerodt asked for his old room. I told him that was occupied and he would have to go in with this man. The room that he was in was a large room—a room with six beds in.

There were other parties in it before these men went there.

Q. Do you know the prisoner, O'Laughlin?

A. No, sir.

Q. You do not remember to have seen him?

A. No.

Q. Did you observe whether either of these parties was armed?'

A. I have seen Atzerodt have a revolver.

Q. On the occasion spoken of?

A. There are others in the party who said he had a knife, but I did not see that.

Q. Did you observe whether the other man, Thomas, as he called himself, was armed?

A. I did not.

Q. You say he stared at you very much; did he make any remark to you?

A. All he said to me was that he was a poor writer.

Q. Did he enter his name himself?

A, I did not see that, but I judge that his name was entered when I came into the room.

Q. You say Atzerodt was in the habit of stopping at your hotel? Had he, on any previous occasion, hesitated to register his name when taking rooms there?

A. No, sir.

Q. You say that he did hesitate on this occasion?

A. On this occasion he hesitated somewhat.

Q. You speak of having seen Atzerodt armed. When was that?

A. That must have been in March, when I first saw his revolver. He had just bought it, and he came in and made the remark that he had just bought it, and I told him I wished I had known that he wanted one, for I could have sold him one that I had—a new one, which I had traded a small one for, and I had no use for it.

Q. Did he exhibit the revolver to you?

A. It was put in my care—handed in to the office.

Q. Do you think you would recognize it if you saw it again?

A. I think I would.

Q. [Exhibiting the revolver identified by John Lee as found in a room at the Kirkwood House.] Is that it?

A. I would not be certain. I do not think it is the same one, but it is something similar.

Cross-examined by Mr. Doster:

Q. Will you be kind enough to state on what day before the 14th of April Atzerodt left your house?

A. It must have been on Wednesday, the 12th.

Q. How long had he stayed at your house at that time?

A. He stayed from the 18th of March until, I think, the 27th. If I had my register I could tell.

Q. I only want to know about the last visit before the 14th of April. How long was he at your house then?

A. He was away for several days—from Wednesday until Saturday morning, between 2 and 3 o'clock.

Q. You say he left on Wednesday, the 12th. How long had he been there before he left on that Wednesday; do you remember?

A. He had been there from the 18th of March. He had been away but once, and then he told me that he was going to the country, and he stayed over night and returned the next day, with a man named Bailey, when he came to the house.

Q. You say that you know of Atzerodt having had interviews with Booth? Can you tell about how many they had?

A. I cannot tell exactly, but quite a number.

Q. Were you present at any of them?

A. No, sir.

Q. Where were these interviews?

A. In front of my house.

Q. On the street?

A. Sometimes on the pavement, sometimes below my house, down towards the National, I have seen them stand.

Q. Were their interviews held in secret in any room?

A. No, sir; I never saw Booth in any room.

Q. You mentioned before that Atzerodt had, previous to this last visit, had arms in his possession?

A. I saw them once; that was when he handed them into the office there.

Q. And you kept them for him?

A. Yes, until he called for them.

Q. Could you or could you not recognize them again?

A. I could not swear to them.

Q. What were the arms?

A. A large revolver, something similar to the one shown me.

Q. What else?

A. Nothing else that I saw.

Q. Did he have a knife?

A. Other persons there say they have seen him with a knife, but I never saw it.

Q. You have mentioned that Atzerodt boasted that on some day he would have enough gold and silver to keep him all his life. What led to that remark? Do you remember the conversation that preceded it?

A. I came into the room; he was drinking at the time; he asked me to take a drink; I took a drink; he paid the bill, and then he said, "Greenawalt, I am pretty near broke, but I have always got friends enough to give me as much money as will see me through."

Q. Did you not have gold and silver in your hand, and shake it in his face?

A. No, sir.

Q. Did any one of the company have gold and silver there?

A. Not that I remember, and not that I saw. I have had half a dollar in my pocket, and I might have had that out, but I do not remember having it out.

Q. Do you not remember saying that you had bought some gold that morning?

A. No, sir.

Q. Had you also been drinking?

A I had taken a drink; I was not in liquor.

Q. Do I understand you to say that you do not remember saying that you had bought gold and silver that morning?

A. I do not remember that I did. When Mr. Bailey left my house, he wanted to pay his stage fare, and I bought some eight or nine $2½ gold pieces, and I do not remember the exact amount of silver, but some $7, I think.

Q. What brought the conversation to gold and silver?

A. I do not know that I ever had any conversation about gold and silver. There was only the remark of Atzerodt; there was no other conversation about it.

Q. Had you not before been talking about money in some shape?

A. No, sir; I had not been talking with him at all until I entered the room. He asked me to drink.

Q. Had any one else, to your knowledge, been talking with him about money?

A. No, sir.

Q. You mentioned a man by the name of Thomas as having come to your house on the morning of this Saturday, between two and three o'clock, in company with Atzerodt. Did they seem to be intimate?

A. No, sir.

Q. Did you take them to be previously acquainted?

A. I could not tell in regard to that. They came to my house.

Q. You can tell what you took them to be. Did you take them to be acquaintances or strangers?

A. I thought they were in company by the way they came there.

Q. Did they look as though they had known one another previously, or had met one another on the street, and just happened to come to your house together?

A. I judged that they were acquainted.

Q. You say this man exhibited signs of disguise? What were they?

A. He had on broadcloth clothing. It did not look like working clothing, and it was well worn—not laboring man's clothing.

Q. His clothing was well worn and broadcloth, and that made you think he was in disguise?

A. Yes, sir.

Q. You have also mentioned that Atzerodt hesitated to register his name? In what shape did he hesitate?

A. "Well," said he, "do you wish my name?" I said, "Certainly." He stood back, and then he walked forward and stopped, and then followed it up and put down his name.

Q. Is it an unusual thing for men to hesitate, when they come there at two or three o'clock in the morning, to register their names?

A. I have not been receiving any guests at that hour. I never had any one to besitate about registering.

Q. Did he say he would not like to do it?

A. No, sir.

Q. Did he seem sleepy?

A. No, he did not, to my knowledge.

Q. Did he seem in liquor?

A. No, he was not in liquor.

Q. Did he seem wide awake?

A. He did.

Q. Do you recognize among the prisoners at the bar the stranger by the name of Thomas?

A. There [pointing to Edward Spangler] is a man who resembles him somewhat. It appears to me he is not as dark. He has not got the beard on he had then. His hair was longer, and, I think, darker. I could not be positive as to that man.

Q. His hair was longer and darker?

A. Yes, sir; and cut down half over his ears. I think he was heavier.

Q. Still you would not swear this was the man?

A. No, sir.

Q. That man stayed with you until five o'clock in the morning?

A. He left about that time, as I understand.

Q. Did you have a conversation with Atzerodt about where he was going in the morning?

A. No, sir; I did not have any conversation with him that morning, no more than I asked him whether he had got back. That was all the conversation that I passed with with him, except that I asked him to register.

Q. After he registered, and while he was registering, he remarked that he was a poor writer?

A. No, sir; Thomas made that remark.

Q. [Exhibiting to the witness the coat identified by John Lee as having been found in the room at the Kirkwood House.] Look at the coat. Do you remember ever having seen that in the possession of Atzerodt?

A. I never did.

Cross-examined by Mr. EWING:

Q. Describe the color of the moustache that the man had on who you say resembled Spangler.

A. Dark, black.

Q. Heavy moustache?

A. Yes, sir.

Q. Had no other whisker?

A. Yes, sir; I think his beard was cut down at the sides.

Q. Was the beard on the side of the face close?

A. His beard came front, and was cut down from the moustache up, but it was either that way or whiskers all around. I knew he had whiskers in front.

Q. What sort of a hat did he wear?

A. A dark slouch hat.

Q. Worn?

A. Yes, sir.

By the Judge Advocate:

Q. Do I understand you to say that you are certain you have not seen the prisoner O'Laughlin at your house?

A. I am. I do not know the man.

By Mr. Doster:

Q. Did I understand you to say that Thomas came in company with Atzerodt?

A. I did not see them come in. When I first saw them Atzerodt was lying on the settee and Thomas standing at the counter at the register.

Q. What made you think they belonged together?

A. The servant told me they came in together.

Q. That is the only ground of your believing they were intimate?

A. That is all I had.

Q. Will you state, if you please, the direct color of the hair and beard of Thomas?

A. As near as I can tell, his hair was black, black eye-brows, and black whiskers. He had a moustache cut off from sides rather close, and beard in front.

Q. Did either the hair or moustache appear to be dyed?

A. No, sir.

Q. What was the color?

A. Black.

Q. Did not Atzerodt refuse or object to this stranger going into his room?

A. No, sir.

Q. Did he ask that he should come in?

A. No, sir.

Q. He simply acceded to it when you told him that there was no other room?

A. Yes, sir. I told him he would have to room with that man.

Q. You forced them together, in short?

A. I told him he would have to. That was my work. I would not force him; he could have taken that or left the house; that was the best I could do for him.

By the Court:

Q. Do you know whether they got up at the same time in the morning?

A. I do not.

Q. Did they occupy the same bed?

A. No.

Q. You said that the last time Atzerodt left your house before the assassination was on Wednesday?

A. I think so. He told me, going away, "Greenawalt, I owe you a couple of days' board; will it make any difference to you

whether I pay for it now or when I come back? I said, "No." Then he remarked, "It will be more convenient for me to pay when I come back." He said he was going to Montgomery county.

Q. Do you know the man that they call O'Laughlin here?

A. No, sir.

Q. Do you know the man with the black moustache, there in the centre of the prisoners' dock, [referring to O'Laughlin.]

A. I do not know him.

Q. You say the man Thomas stared at you at one time?

A. Yes, sir; when I entered the room he did.

Q. Was that in the light?

A. Rather a dim light—about half the jet of gas burning—one burner.

Q. Did you have a distinct view of his face then?

A. I had a fair view of him.

Q. Do you recognize that face among the prisoners at the bar?

A. I do not—not that I could swear to.

Q. Did you see the color of his eyes, his hair, his complexion?

A. He had dark eyes, dark complexion.

Q. What was his beard?

A. Black.

A. B. OLIN,

a witness called for the prosecution, being duly sworn, testified as follows:

By the Judge Advocate:

Q. Judge, will you state to the Court whether or not, on the morning of the 15th of April, you visited Ford's Theatre and inspected the President's box, as it is called there.

A. Sunday following the 16th I first visited the theatre. The assassination was on the evening of the 14th, and on the 15th I was engaged in taking depositions.

Q. Will you state the examination which you made, and the condition in which you found the box, and doors, and locks?

A. My attention was called to the incision into the wall that was prepared to receive the brace that fitted into the corner of the panel of the door; the brace was not there.

Q. That is the outer door you speak of?

A. The door entering the alley way into the box which crossed the alley at an angle with the wall, and a brace fitted against the wall to the corner of the door fastens the door very securely. I discovered that, and looked for the remains of the plastering that had been cut from the wall to make this incision. That was all, so far as I could observe, carefully removed from a little carpet, where it must have fallen, as it was cut by some sharp instrument. That plastering was all carefully removed.

It was said to me that the pistol was discharged through the panel of the door. The

passage-way is somewhat dark, and I procured a light and examined very carefully the hole bored through the door. I discovered at once that the hole was made by some small instrument in the first place, and was. as I supposed, cut out then by a sharp instrument like a penknife; and you can see, by placing a light near the door—if I am not very much mistaken, I thought I saw—marks of a sharp cutting knife, cleaning out every obstacle to looking through that hole in the door. I then discovered, also, that the clasp that fastens the bolt of the first door—this would be a double box on some occasions, there is a movable partition fitted to it—on the clasp that receives the lock of that door, the upper screw holding the clasp had been loosened in such a way that when the door was locked, by putting my forefinger against the door and pushing it, I could push the door open.

I seated myself as near as I could ascertain the position of the chair in which the President sat that evening; for I procured, to accompany me, Miss Harris, who I understood was in the box on that occasion, and she located the chair as nearly as she recollected it to have been placed on the evening; and in seating myself in the chair, closing that door, and letting a person place his eye very near that hole, close to the door, the range would be about from one to the other, striking my head about midway from the base to the crown.

I directed my attention principally at that early stage of the investigation to ascertaining more particularly the precise period of the occurrence, as there was some uncertainty at that time whether the attack upon Mr. Seward's family and the assassination of the President was the result of the act of some one person or more persons, and I directed my attention in the first place more particularly to ascertaining the precise period of time as nearly as I could when this occurred. I continued to make some examinations.

Q. Did you examine the condition of the locks on the doors?

A. I did. I examined the condition of the locks. The lock played readily.

Q. A hasp or catch?

A. As I before observed, the catch of one door, the first door that would enter into the first box as you passed into the box from this alley-way, the upper screw holding the hasp was loosened in such a way that it could be pressed upon with the finger when the door was locked, and the hasp would fall back. I also examined to see if I could discover the chips that must have been made by boring and cutting out this small hole, but they had apparently been removed. I discovered nothing of them.

Q. Did you see the bar, or had it been lost?

A. It had been removed by some one. You could see the indentation upon the door, in the panel of the door, where some brace might have been made from the wall to the door. That indentation there is perceptible, and the brace was so fixed in that it would be very difficult to remove it from the outside. I do not think it could be done without breaking the door down. The more pressure that was made from the dress circle of the theatre upon that bar, the firmer it would have been held in its place; but it was securely fastened in its place, for it rested on that hole in the wall and the panel of the door.

Q. Did it bear the appearance of having been recently made?

A. Yes, sir. It was a freshly cut hole. The wood was as fresh as it would have been the instant it was cut, apparently, to the observation.

Q. Can you describe the chair?

A. It is a large, high-backed arm-chair and satin cushions.

Q. A rocking-chair?

A. I think not a rocking-chair. From nearly opposite the place where the President's head might have rested against the chair, I think I could discover, although it was red, the marks of several drops of blood.

By Mr. AIKEN:

Q. Are the civil courts of this District in full and free operation?

A. They are in operation; at least, they were before I adjourned one to-day.

By Mr. DOSTER:

Q. Will you be kind enough to state whether the civil courts are supposed to sit by the consent of and in order to carry out the will of Gen. Grant?

A. I really do not know how anybody supposes that. He has given me no information on that subject.

MAJOR HENRY R. RATHBONE, recalled.

By the JUDGE ADVOCATE:

Q. After the shot had been fired, did you go to the outer door of the President's box, and examine how it was closed?

A. I did, sir; for the purpose of calling medical aid.

Q. In what condition did you find it?

A. I found the door barred, so that the people who were knocking on the outside could not gain an entrance.

Q. Did you make an attempt to remove the bar?

A. I did, sir; and removed it with difficulty.

Q. Was that after you had received the stab from the assassin?

A. Yes, sir.

[Exhibiting a bar to the witness.] Is that blood on that wooden bar from your arm?

A. I am not able to say that; but my wound was bleeding freely at the time.

Q. In what condition did you find the bar?

A. The bar was securely fastened in the wall, and appeared to be resting against the moulding of the door. I think it could not have been jostled out by any pushing from the outside.

Q. Did you notice particularly the chair in which the President sat? What was its character?

A. Nothing, except that it was a large, easy chair, covered with damask cloth.

Q. You do not know whether it had rockers or not?

A. My impression was that it had; I am not sure.

By the COURT:

Q. Is that the bar the door was closed with?

A. I am not able to say.

Q Was it similar to that?

A. My impression was, that it was a different piece of wood.

ISAAC JAQUETTE,

a witness called for the prosecution, being duly sworn, testified as follows:

By the JUDGE ADVOCATE:

Q. [Exhibiting a bar to the witness.]— Will you please state to the Court whether or not you found that bar in Ford's Theatre, and under what circumstances, and where?

A. Yes, sir. Soon after the President was carried out, I went to the box with several others, and this bar was lying inside of the first door going into the box—lying on the floor. I picked it up. I stayed around there some time, and then carried it out.

Q. Did you take it home with you?

A. Yes, sir.

Q. There has been a piece sawed off, has there not?

A. Yes, sir. There was an officer stopping at the same boarding-house where I was, and he wanted a piece of it. I sawed a piece off, but he concluded not to take it afterwards.

Q. These spots upon it are blood?

A. Yes, sir.

Q. Were they fresh at the time?

A. They looked fresh at the time.

[The bar was offered in evidence without objection.]

JOE SIMMS, (Colored,)

recalled for the prosecution:

By the JUDGE ADVOCATE:

Q. Will you state whether or not you have been working at Ford's Theatre?

A. Yes, sir. I have worked at Mr. Ford's Theatre for two years.

Q. Were you there on the evening of the day on the night of which the President was assassinated?

A. Yes, sir.

Q. Did you see the persons engaged in decorating the President's box that afternoon?

A. Mr. Harry Ford and another gentleman, I do not know his name exactly, were up there fixing up the box. Mr. Harry Ford told me to go up to his bed-room and get a rocking-chair out and bring it down and put it in the President's box. I did so, according to his orders. When I carried the chair into the private box and set it down, Mr. Harry Ford said, "You can go down, that is all I want;" and I immediately passed down the stairs.

Q. You carried it into the box yourself, did you?

A. Yes, sir. He told me to bring it out of his sleeping-room and put it into the private box.

Q. Had it ever been there before?

A. Not this season.

Q. Was it a rocking-chair?

A. Yes, sir.

Q. How was the back, high or low?

A. It was a chair with a high back to it.

Q. And cushioned?

A. Yes, sir.

Q. Did you see the prisoner, Edward Spangler, there on that occasion?

A. Not at that time. There was no one in the box at that time but Mr. Harry Ford and the other gentleman that was helping to fix it. He had started to go down when he told me to go after the chair.

Q. Was Spangler on the stage that afternoon when you were bringing the chair?

A. Mr. Spangler was obliged to be there; he was there all the time.

Q. Was he there that afternoon?

A. He was there that afternoon. He was obliged to be there. There was no other place for him. He worked there altogether, the same as I did, and had no calling away only when he went to his boarding house.

Q. I understood you to say that he was in there when the chair was put in the box?

A. I did not see Mr. Spangler in the private box. I carried it up, but I did not say Mr. Spangler was in there.

Q. Was he on the stage at the time—do you know?

A. He might have been on the stage or somewhere about the building.

Cross-examined by Mr. EWING:

Q. You say Mr. Spangler might have been on the stage then?

A. Yes, sir.

Q. You did not see him then?

A. No, sir; I did not see him. I did not notice particular. When Mr. Harry Ford told me to go up in his room and bring down the chair, of course I went, not noticing particular, which I hardly ever did; I have been there so long at work that I hardly ever notice persons so particular; but this Mr. Spangler had no other calling away in the week, only right at the theatre, on the stage, except when called up to his boarding house.

Q. You say he had no "other calling away." You mean that was all the business he was engaged in?

A. No, sir; that was his business.

Q. You do not know whether he might not have had something to call him away from the theatre just at that time, do you?

A. No, sir; I do not.

Q. Who was this other gentleman that was in the box with Mr. Harry Ford?

A. I think his name is Mr. Buckingham; I may be mistaken.

Q. Was he employed about the theatre?

A. He stood at the doors at night to take the tickets when the people came in; he was doorkeeper in front of the house.

Q. You think it was Mr. Buckingham that was there then with Mr. Harry Ford?

A. I think it was Mr. Buckingham that was helping Mr. Harry Ford to fix up the private box.

Q. What hour in the afternoon was it?

A. It was a little after three o'clock, I think; I did not notice the time particularly; it might have been later and it might have been sooner.

Q. Mr. Ford called you to come up to the box, did he?

A. Yes, sir. I was doing something somewhere around the building, and he called me and told me to go to his room and bring down that large rocking-chair out of his sleeping room and put it in the private box. I did so, according to his order.

Q. Where were you when he called you?

A. I do not know exactly where I was; whether I was out in the alley, or whether I was up on the flies; but I was somewhere about the building, I know, when he called me.

Q. You were near enough to hear when he called?

A. I had come in from carrying bills; I carried the bills out every day so that the people could see what was going to be played; and I came back that evening and was about to take my meal, was going to eat up on the flie, when he called me. He called me down, and told me to go up to his room and get the chair.

Q. You took your meals up on the flies, did you?

A. Yes, sir; I used to take my meals there, of course.

Q. At what time did you generally take that meal?

A. I generally took it whenever I could. When I came in the morning I would take out the bills, and that would keep me sometimes until three o'clock, and sometimes longer; and whenever I would come back I would eat.

Q. And you were eating when he called you?

A. When he called me to bring the chair, I put down my meal, and went and got the chair for him, and put it in the private box.

Q. Did you see Mr. Spangler as you went to the box at all?

A. No, sir; I did not see Mr. Spangler. I did not see him when I went to the box, neither did I see him when I came away from the private box.

Q. Describe that chair.

A. There is not a chair in here like it, but it was one of those high-backed rocking-chairs, with a high cushion on it—a red cushion.

Q. What kind of material was the cushion made of, cloth or satin?

A. A kind of satin.

Q. Do you know that the chair never was in the private box before this season?

A. Not this season that I know of.

Q. When was it in?

A. Last season. When they got it last season it was in the private box, and Mr. Harry Ford told me to take it out of the private box and carry it up in his room. That was the only one up in his room.

Q. It was bought last season?

A. Last season.

Q. Was there any other furniture for the box of the same character?

A. Yes, sir.

Q. What other pieces?

A. There was a sofa and some other chairs.

Q. Any other big chair?

A. Not in that box that I know of. I did not notice particularly. It was not my business to be looking into this place, and therefore I did not notice particularly. I never went in there only when I was sent, for there were persons to clean it up and go all about, and I just attended to the outside work.

Q. Was the sofa covered with the same material?

A. Yes, sir; it was covered with the same material.

Q. Was that furniture bought for the private box?

A. I do not know whether it was bought for the private box, or whether it was bought for the properties, to be used on the stage.

Q. Was it bought for the theatre?

A. Yes, sir.

Q. And it was in the private box last season?

A. Yes, sir; last season.

Q. With the rest of the set that it belonged to?

A. With the rest of the furniture that was in there.

Q. The rest of the furniture you spoke of was covered with the same sort of cloth?

A. Yes, sir.

By the JUDGE ADVOCATE:

Q. Did you take a large chair out of that box at the time you put this one in?

A. No, sir; I did not take one in and one out.

Q. You do not know what kind of a chair was there before?

28

A. No, sir, I do not. I just brought that chair in and set it down. Mr. Ford said, that is all I want with you;" and I went down immediately.

CHARLES H. ROSCH,

a witness called for the prosecution, being duly sworn, testified as follows:

By the JUDGE ADVOCATE:

Q. State whether you know the prisoner Edward Spangler?

A. I do not know him personally.

Q. Do you know him when you see him?

A. No; I was not there at the arrest. I went to his house and secured the rope.

Q. You were not present at his arrest?

A. No, sir.

Q. Did you go to his house after the arrest?

A. Yes, sir.

Q. What did you find there?

A. We found a carpet-bag at the house where he takes his meals, on the corner of Seventh and H streets. The man in charge of the house handed us a carpet-bag, in which we found a piece of rope, which I measured afterwards, and found to contain eighty-one feet, and the twist was very carefully taken out. There was nothing else in the carpet-bag except some blank paper and a dirty shirt collar. When we inquired for his trunk, we were told that he kept it at the theatre.

Q. When was that carpet-bag with the rope left there?

A. It was left at the house where he generally took his meals.

Q. When?

A. That I do not know.

Q. When did you take it?

A. I took that rope from the house on the evening of Monday, the 17th of April since, between nine and ten o'clock, in company with two military detectives.

Q. Who were with you?

A. Two of the Provost Marshal's detectives.

Q. Do you know their names?

A. I do not.

Q. You did not see Spangler himself then?

A. I did not. I was to have gone with the other officers for the purpose of securing papers, but I missed them, and consequently I was not present when he was arrested.

Q. Did you find the carpet-bag open? Had it been open?

A. No, sir; we made out to open it between us. It was locked. We found keys to unlock it.

Cross-examined by Mr. EWING:

Q. Where is the house at which you got the carpet-bag?

A. It is on the northwest corner of Seventh and H streets.

Q. Who gave it to you?

A. We took it when we found that it belonged to Spangler.

Q. Who was there?

A. A man called Jake, who works at the theatre in company with Spangler, told me that was Spangler's carpet sack, and that that was all he had at that house.

Q. What was the man's name?

A. He is commonly called Jake; that is all I know; he is apparently a German.

Q. What persons in the house that lived or stayed there did you see?

A. A couple of the boarders, I presume they were. I did not know any of the other parties that were in the house.

Q. What room was it that you got it out of?

A. The bed-room up stairs.

Q. What part of the house?

A. As near as I could judge, on the south side.

Q. On the south side of the house?

A. Yes; the room was facing to the south.

Q. Describe the room.

A. It was on the north side of the room itself where the bag was, right near where Jake —the man I referred to—had his trunk. He was working, as he said, in the same theatre with Spangler.

Q. Look at that coil of rope, and state whether or not it is the same that you found in Spangler's carpet-bag.

A. I am satisfied and believe that is the same rope.

Q. What did you do with the monkey-wrench?

A. I found no monkey-wrench in that carpet-bag.

Q. Did you find any anywhere else?

A. No, sir.

The witness added: I beg leave of the Court to correct my statement as to the locality of the house, not being fully posted as to the latitude. Since reflecting on it, I think it is the northeast corner of Seventh and H streets.

By Assistant Judge Advocate BURNETT:

Q. On what floor is the room?

A. On the second floor.

Q. Was the room numbered?

A. Where we were taken to, where the carpet-bag was found, there was no number on the room.

WILLIAM EATON

recalled by the prosecution.

By the JUDGE ADVOCATE:

Q. State to the Court whether or not you arrested the prisoner Edward Spangler?

A. I did.

Q. At what day, and under what circumstances?

A. I do not recollect the date.

Q. State the day as near as you can?

A. I cannot state the date. It was the next week after the assassination.

Q. Where did you arrest him?

A. In a house on Seventh street, near the Patent Office.

Q. The corner of Seventh and which street was it?

A. I think it is between G and H.

Q. Was it at the corner of Seventh and H?

A. It was.

Q. Which corner? Can you state?

A. The right-hand side of Seventh street.

Q Is it the northeast corner or not?

A. It must be the southeast corner.

Q. Do you know whose house it is?

A. I do not.

Q. Did you find any weapons in his possession?

A. No, sir; I did not search him. My orders were to arrest him.

Q. Was that his boarding-house?

A. I think it was.

Q. Who was with him?

A. I do not know—the ladies who were in the house.

Q. Are you certain as to the corner on which that house stands? Reflect and see whether you are right in your recollection.

A. I know it is in the corner building; I do not know whether it is on the corner door.

Q. Is it on the northeast or southeast corner?

A. I think it is on the southeast corner. No cross-examination.

James J. Gifford,

a witness called for the prosecution, being duly sworn, testified as follows:

By the Judge Advocate:

Q. Will you state to the Court whether or not you have been connected with Ford's Theatre, in this city?

A. Yes, sir.

Q. In what capacity?

A. I was the builder of it.

Q. In what capacity afterwards?

A. I have taken care of the building, keeping it in order, and working on the stage.

Q. You have been the carpenter there?

A. Yes, sir.

Q. Were you the carpenter there on the 14th and 15th of April last?

A. Yes, sir.

Q. Did you observe the President's box in the theatre on that day?

A. No, sir; I did not look at it that day; I was not in it.

Q. Do you know who decorated that box on that occasion?

A. I saw Mr. Harry Clay Ford in the box putting flags out.

Q. Who else?

A. At one time I saw Mr. Raybold, I think, with him; I am not certain.

Q. Anybody else?

A. No, sir.

Q. Did you see the prisoner Spangler in the box at any time during that day?

A. No, sir; I did not.

Q. Did you observe a large rocking-chair which was in the President's box in the theatre on the 14th of April?

A. I observed it afterwards; I did not take notice of it on the 14th.

Q. When did you see it?

A. I saw it on Saturday, the 15th.

Q. Where?

A. In the box.

Q. Do you know when it was placed in the box?

A. No, sir.

Q. Nor by whom?

A. No, sir.

Q. Do you know whether it had ever been there before?

A. I do not think it had been this season. I saw it there last season.

Q. To whom did it belong, and where had it come from?

A. It belonged to Mr. John T. Ford. It was a part of a set of furniture—two sofas and two high-backed chairs, one with rockers and one with castors; I have sometimes seen the one with castors in the box this season, but I never saw the rocking-chair in it. The last I saw of the chair before this was in Mr. James R. Ford's and Henry Clay Ford's room.

Q. In the theatre?

A. Adjoining the theatre.

Q. You say it had not been in the box in the theatre during the past season?

A. Not this season that I have seen. I saw it last season, not this season.

Q. When did you see it in Ford's room?

A. I suppose it must be three or four or five weeks before the occurrence.

Q. When did you see it again?

A. Not until Saturday morning, April 15th.

B. Did you see it after that anywhere?

A. No, sir; except on Sunday and Monday, when I came away from there.

Q. Do you know who took it away?

A. No, sir.

Q. Do you know whether the scenes of the theatre remain as they were the moment of the assassination?

A. I set a scene there for a gentleman to take a view for the Secretary of War. At the time I left the theatre the scene was then set as it was the night of the assassination. The back flats in the three back grooves had been pushed off. I do not know whether they were pushed back since. They had been pushed off so as to give a view for the occupants of the side box. I pushed them off the box to assist in making the pictures.

Q. Have you examined the condition of the locks on the doors of that box?

A. No, sir; I have not.

Q. Did you examine the wall where there is a mortise made?

A. Yes, sir.

Q. When did you examine that first?

A. No. sir: I do not.

Cross-examined by Mr. EWING:

Q. [Submitting to the witness a plan of the theatre.] Will you examine that plat carefully, and state whether it is or is not an approximately correct plat of the theatre?

A. The lines in the orchestra are not correct. They are all curved lines; these are straight lines.

Q. [Exhibiting another plan of the theatre to the witness.] Examine this map and state if you think it to be correct?

A. The front line of this plan is not correct. The side line on the south side is not correct.

Q. State in what it is incorrect?

A. This line on the stage curves out. It is just the reverse of what the gentleman who drew this has intended for it. Then on the south side there is a projection of about three feet. The stage is that much narrower on that side than it is on the other, and that much narrower than the front of the house.

Q. State what other defects, if any, you see in that map.

A. The fronts of the private boxes are straight; in this they have got a sweep. On the centre on the east wall there is a very large opening, some fourteen feet, which is not marked here at all. Those are all the defects I see in it at present. I do not know what is the meaning of these lines on one side, unless they are intended for packs of scenes. The scenes are as they were when I left it. There are three packs here.

Q. They appear to represent the scenes as they were when you last saw them?

A. Yes, sir.

Q. State whether, in other respects, the map is substantially correct in your opinion?

A. It shows the grooves and the entrances all correctly. The only difference in that respect is that they have made the first entrance a little smaller in proportion to the others in laying them down. I do not know the scale of this drawing and therefore cannot tell.

[The map was offered in evidence without objection.]

Q. How wide is the first entrance?

A. About four feet six inches.

Q. Is that the entrance by which Booth passed off from the stage behind the scenes?

A. That is the way they told me he passed; that is the entrance he must have gone through.

Q. How wide is the passage-way that he passed through going to the outer door?

A. I judge it is from about two feet eight inches to three feet; in some places a little wider, and some a little narrower. It is not a regular straight entrance.

Q. Now tell the Court as to whether that passage-way is obstructed during the plays, ordinarily?

A. Never, except by people when they have a large company on the small stage. There are never any chairs or tables or scenery put in the way there, so that they can have free access to go under the stage and come up on the other side.

Q. Is it not also necessary to keep the passage way clear to allow the actors and actresses to pass without obstruction from the green-room and the dressing-rooms on to the stage?

A. Yes, sir; that is what it is intended for.

Q. How is the small back door usually kept?

A. It is always left open until the performance is over, and then it is locked until morning.

R. Do you mean that the door is swung open, or left unlocked merely?

A. It is left unlocked. The only door that is locked is the door leading from the stage to the front of the house on the side underneath the box where the President was assassinated.

Q. State what position upon the stage Mr. Spangler had during a performance?

A. His business was on the left hand of the stage—the right hand from the audience—to run the flats, as we call them, on that side.

Q. Was that the side the President's box was on?

A. Yes, sir.

Q. State at what times during the performance you were on the stage that night?

A. I was on the stage until the curtain went up at each act. When the curtain was down I would go around on to the stage, to see that everything was right, and then go out again.

Q. State at what times during that evening, when you came on the stage between the acts, you saw Mr. Spangler?

A. I could not state the time. I should judge the last time I saw him was at about half-past nine o'clock.

Q. State whether you saw him each time you came on the stage.

A. Yes, sir; I saw him each time.

Q. He was your subordinate, I believe?

A. Yes, sir.

Q. State where you were during that play when you were not on the stage.

A. I was in the front of the house. I walked down to D and Tenth streets to look at a big lamp I had put up there, while the first act was going on. I walked up to the next corner, Tenth and F streets, and took a glass of ale, and stood and talked a moment or two, during the second act. During the third act I did not leave the house at all.

Q. You were then in front of the theatre a part of the time between the second and third acts?

A. Yes, sir.

Q. How much of the time?

A. I was on the stage between the acts.

Q. You were in front of the theatre during the performance of the second act?

A. During the performance of the second act I was in front, I think, to the best of my knowledge.

Q. All the time?

A. No, sir; not all the time.

Q. How much of the time?

A. I do not know. I would walk in and maybe stay five or ten minutes and then walk out again.

Q. State whether or not you saw the prisoner Spangler at any time during that play in front of the theatre?

A. I did not see him in front of the theatre. I do not think he could have been there in front of the theatre without my knowing it, because the scenes would have gone wrong if he had left the stage any length of time.

Q. Did you ever see Spangler wear a moustache?

A. No, sir; he has never worn one since I have known him.

Q. Do you know how he was dressed that evening?

A. No, sir; I do not; I did not take particular notice.

Q. How was he ordinarily dressed during that period?

A. Just about the same as he is now, as far as I have seen. Lately, during the last four or five weeks, he has been wearing the clothes he has on now.

Q. Was not the play of the American Cousin a play in which the scenes were shifted a good deal?

A. They were what we call "plain-sailing," running-on scenes. There is but one set scene in the piece.

Q. There was not much shifting, then?

A. In one act the most of the scenes are changed; but that is in the first groove, and, therefore, it only takes two men to change them until we get to two, and then it takes four men.

Q. Were the scenes shifted much in the play?

A. I believe there are some five or six scenes in each act. I do not know—I cannot call to mind now—how many scenes are in each act.

Q. Then Spangler's presence there would have been indispensable to the performance?

A. Yes, sir. If he had not been there his scene would not have gone on.

Q. Who was with him on duty on that side that night?

A. Ritterspaugh—I think that is the name —was with him at that time.

Q. Did you hear Booth call Spangler that night?

A. No, sir.

Q. What was Spangler's connection with Booth—what had he to do with him?

A. Nothing that I know of, further than

friendly. Everybody about the house was friendly with him.

Q. With Booth?

A. Yes, sir; actors and all; they were all friendly with him. He had such a very winning way that it made every person like him. He was a good-natured and jovial kind of man. The people about the house, as far as I knew, all liked him.

Q. Was he not very much in the habit of frequenting the theatre?

A. Sometimes I have seen him there for a week, and then he would go off, and I would not see him for a couple of weeks. Then he would come again for a week, perhaps, and after that I would not see him for a couple of weeks, or ten days, or something of that sort.

Q. Did he not have access to the theatre as one of the employees would have?

A. Yes, sir.

Q. And had access by the back entrance?

A. Yes, sir.

Q. At any time?

A. Yes, sir; at any time except when the door was locked.

Q. At any time when an employee of the theatre might go in?

A. When the house was open he had free access all through the house.

Q. Day and night?

A. Yes, sir; except when the house was locked up and the watchman was there; he had no access to it then.

Q. Was not Spangler a sort of a drudge for Booth?

A. He appeared so; he used to go down and help him to hitch his horse up, and such things, I am told; I have seen him once or twice hitching the horse up myself.

Q. Was that hole in the wall cut into the brick?

A. No, sir, I believe not; it was only cut into the plaster, I should judge, about an inch or an inch and an eighth.

Q. You say it might have been done with a penknife?

A. Yes, sir; I think it might have been done with a penknife.

Q. [Submitting to the witness the wooden bar heretofore offered in evidence, marked Exhibit No. 44.] Will you examine that stick and state whether you saw any sticks like that about the theatre about that time?

A. No, sir, I did not; this is the first time I have seen anything of this kind.

Q. State whether those nails in the end would probably have been put in there for any purpose connected with the fastening of the door?

A. They might have been put in there to keep it from slipping down—one end against the wall, and the other with the bevelled edge against the moulding of the door.

Q. State whether the nails in that end, [a detached piece which had been sawed off

the wooden bar,] would probably have been put in for any purpose connected with that object.

A. I do not know what they could have been done for.

Q. You think they could not, in any way, have facilitated that object?

A. They might have. If this strip was too short, this block would fit in behind there so as to make an abutment for it.

Q. But that was a part of the stick; it was on the stick, and was sawed off by a curiosity-hunter. Would these nails have been put in there for any purpose connected with the fastening of the door?

A. No, sir; I see no use for them there. This bevelled edge would keep it from slipping down the door, and the other end being in the mortise, it would not require anything to keep it from slipping down.

Q. How long would it have taken, with an ordinary penknife, to cut that hole in the wall you speak of?

A. I should suppose a man intent on mischief would do it in some ten or fifteen minutes. After the face of the plastering is broken, the sand and lime runs out very easy.

Q. I believe you have said that you do not know how the lock on the door of the President's box came to be loose?

A. No, sir, I do not.

Q. When did you first hear that the President was coming to the theatre that night?

A. I judge it was between eleven and twelve o'clock.

Q. Do you know whether he was invited to the theatre?

A. I do not know.

MAY 22.

JACOB RITTERSPAUGH,

a witness called for the prosecution, being duly sworn, testified as follows:

By Assistant Judge Advocate BINGHAM:

Q. Do you know the prisoner, Edward Spangler?

A. I do.

Q. Do you know where he lived in Washington until he was arrested?

A. He boarded where I board.

Q. Where was that?

A. Mrs. Scott's, on the corner of Seventh and G streets.

Q. Who arrested him?

A. I do not know, I was not there at the time he was arrested.

Q. What is the name of the house?

A. I do not know; there is no number on the house.

Q. Who owns it?

A. A Mr. Ford, I think.

Q. Does he live in it?

A. No, sir; Mrs. Scott has it leased from Mr. Ford.

Q. Who lives in the house?

A. Mrs. Scott.

Q. Who occupied the room with Spangler?

A. He never slept there; he just took his meals; that was all.

Q. Did he have a room in the house?

A. No, sir; he slept at the theatre.

Q. Did you see the rope that was taken there?

A. No, sir; I know he had a valise there; he used to keep it there. I do not know whether anything was in it or not. The detectives came in and asked me if Spangler had anything there, and I told them I did not know any more than the valise, and I gave it to them, and they took it and went off with it.

Q. You know that that valise that you gave them was Spangler's valise.

A. Yes, sir.

Q. You do not know what it contained?

A. No, sir; I have never looked into it.— They took it off. They asked me if he had any chests or trunks, and I told them no; he had no clothes there or anything else.

Q. When did he bring the valise there?

A. I do not know.

Q. When did you give it to the officers?

A. On Monday night, the 17th of April last.

Q. Are you not commonly called "Jake" about the theatre?

A. I am.

JOSEPH B. STEWART,

a witness called for the prosecution, being duly sworn, testified as follows:

By the JUDGE ADVOCATE:

Q. State to the Court whether or not you were at Ford's Theatre on the night of the assassination of the President?

A. I was.

Q. State whether or not you saw the assassin leap from the President's box upon the stage?

A. I did.

Q. Did you, or not, follow him? State the circumstances of your pursuit.

A. I did not follow him. At about near half-past ten, I was sitting in the front seat of the orchestra on the right-hand side. There are two aisles in the orchestra. My seat was the one forming the corner seat on the left-hand side of the right-hand aisle, which would bring me immediately next to the music-stand. The report of a pistol, which was evidently a charged pistol—a sharp report— startled me. I was talking at the moment to my sister, who sat by me, my head leaning to the left. I glanced still further left and immediately back to the stage, and at the same time an exclamation was made, and simultaneously a man leaped from the President's box alighting on the stage, exclaiming, as he came out, some words which I understood. He came down with his back slightly to the audience, but rising and turning, his face came in full view. At the same instant I rose up and attempted to leap on the stage directly from where I sat. My foot slipped from the rail. My eye, at the same time, discovered the distance, and, without stopping my motion at all, I turned and made two or three steps on the railing and jumped on the stage to the right of the foot lights where I sat, keeping my attention all the time, after selecting my course, upon the man who was crossing the stage, and who had just jumped from the President's box. When I reached the stage, as I was reaching it, looking in an angle to the left, I perceived that he disappeared at the same instant around the left-hand stage entrance. Being on the stage, I crossed it as quick as possible. I had never been on the stage, and knew nothing about the condition of the building or the means of exit; but I supposed the person was getting out, and I followed the direction he took. I exclaimed, "Stop that man" three times. The last time, and when I had passed the length of the stage and turned to the right, and when I suppose within a distance of from twenty to twenty-five feet from the door, the door slammed decidedly—came to, closed. I was going just as fast as I could, and got to the door of course very quickly. Coming against the door, I touched it first on the side where it did not open. I then caught hold of the door at the proper point, opened it, and passed out. The last time that I exclaimed, "Stop that man," some one said, "He is getting on a horse;" and at the door, almost as soon as the words reached my ears, I heard the tramping of a horse. On opening the door after the balk at the door which prevented me from opening it at first, I perceived a man mounting a horse. He was at that instant rather imperfectly mounted; the moon was just beginning to rise, and I could see a little elevated better than I could immediately down to the ground. The horse was moving in a quick, agitated motion, as a horse will do if prematurely spurred in mounting with the rein drawn a little to one side; and for a moment the horse described a kind of a circle from the right to the left, which I noticed. I noticed at the same time that there were on the left some tenement houses. I ran in the direction where the horse was heading, and when within eight or ten feet of the head of the horse, and almost up within reach of the left flank of the horse, the rider brought him around somewhat in a similar circle from the left to the right again, crossing over, the horse's feet rattling violently on what seemed to be rocks. I crossed in the same direction, aiming at the rein, and was now on the right flank of the horse. He was rather gaining on me then, though not yet in a forward movement. I could have reached his flank myself with my hand when perhaps two-thirds of the way over the alley. Again he backed to the right-

hand side of the alley, brought the horse forward and spurred him, and at the same instant crouched forward down over the pommel of the saddle, and the horse went forward then and soon swept to the left up towards F street. I still ran after the horse some forty or fifty yards. I commanded the person to stop in the alley. The horse went on rapidly after starting forward. It all occupied a space of a few seconds from the time I reached the stage until this occurred.

Q. You say you found the door closed; did you see anybody standing about the door?

A. I did.

Q. One or more persons?

A. I passed several person in that passage way, ladies and gentlemen—one or two men; I think in all perhaps five persons, as near as I could estimate without being able to count them. Near the door on my right hand side I passed a person standing, who seemed to be in the act of turning. I was noticing everything that came before me, as I was impressed with what had occurred, and I saw a person who did not seem to be moving about like the others. Every one else I saw but that one person was in a terrible commotion and moving about.

Q. Could you describe that person's appearance; do you think you would recognize him again?

A. I would not like to undertake to recognize him positively, but I have a very distinct impression in my mind about the size and appearance of that man.

Q. Look at the prisoners here and say whether either of them, in your opinion, is that person?

A. I know none of these prisoners, and I see but one face among them there that would call to mind that person.

Q. Which is that?

A. There it is, [pointing to Edw'd Spangler.]

Q. Is that the person?

A. That man looks more like the person I saw near the door than anybody else I see there. He makes the impression of the man's visage as I caught it as I was going along very rapidly.

Q. Describe his bearing.

A. As I approached the door, about as far as from here to the wall of this room, [indicating a distance of about fifteen feet,] the person who was at the door was facing towards the door; but as I got nearer he turned around partially, so that I had a view of him. The view I had was the view of a person turning a quarter, describing three-quarters of a circle, as he turned, and the size and visage were observed so far as to leave on my mind an impression of the visage.

Q. Was he turning away from the door?

A. Turning from the door, and towards me.

Cross-examined by Mr. Ewing:

Q. There is a passage-way between the scenes and the green-room, about two and a half or three feet in width, through which Booth ran as he passed out of the door. Was it in that passage-way that you met this person, or was it between the scenes?

A. I do not know where the green-room is. I never was on the stage before If I had a diagram of the building, I could point out the spot.

Q. [Submitting to the witness the diagram heretofore offered in evidence and marked Exhibit No. 48.] This is a plan of the theatre ; now describe the locality.

A. When I was coming through the passage from the front of the stage to the door I saw a person near the side door, as I advanced in that direction rapidly, and I observed a person standing at the outer door, who, as I have described, was turning from the right to the left when I noticed him. It was in what you may call the passage—the one that leads from the front to the rear of the theatre, after passing over the stage and turning to the right—going towards the small door.

Q. About how far from the door did the man stand?

A. About three feet.

Q. Did you notice him there just after the door closed?

A. Just after it slammed. I was approaching the door. It was my expectation when I reached the stage to catch the person who had jumped from the President's box, inside of the house or very soon after he should get out of it, and I was watching very closely every person whom I approached.

Q. If this man had been the person who slammed the door would you have noticed him doing it?

A. No, sir. A person standing in that position could, by a reach of the arm, have slammed the door, and I could not have noticed it.

Q. But would not that have thrown him around?—would it not have given him a motion different from the motion that he was making as you approached?

A. I recollect well the action of the door. It is a narrow door—not a wide door. Approaching it, it opens inwards to the right as you approach. When I came against the door, I came with my hand, and somewhat damaged my hand against a part of the hinge. The door was very narrow, and any one standing in that man's position could have slammed the door very easily by reaching his hand to it.

Q. Which way does the door open—towards the side that the President was on, or from the side that the President was on?

A. Approaching the door from the stage to the rear, it hinges from the right to the left. Entering it from the outside, it would swing back from the left to the right to the inside. I came violently against the door when I went to open it.

Q. That is the lock of the door, when the door was shut, was on the side nearest the side on which the President sat?

A. If you will give me a slip of paper, I will describe the way the door stood.

Mr. Ewing. The Court has been there.

The Witness. Then they will understand me. The lock of the door, approaching it, was on my right-hand side, the hinge to the left. Not knowing which side it swung on, I came against it on the left, and therefore I had to change my position before I could get out. If the door had been opened, so that I would not have been stopped at it, I could have got the range of that horse outside.

Q. But the person you speak of, who, you think, resembles the prisoner Spangler, as you approached towards the door, was turning from left to right?

A. No, the other way. The door being on his right-hand side, he was turning to the left.

Q. Had he his back towards the door?

A. His right side stood quarter-face to the door, coming towards me.

Q. His body was moving around from the door and towards you?

A. Yes, from the door.

Q. That is not the motion that the movement of shutting the door would gradually give to the body, is it.

A. That would be owing to which hand the door was shut with.

Q. With either hand?

A. With the right hand it might or might not.

Q. Where were you in in the passage when you noticed that person—how far down the passage had you got?

A. I noticed him in about the second stride I made after I heard the door slam. At the moment the door did slam I had just passed one person ; and then one or two more, in a great deal of agitation, came out within the passage-way, and I am sure that not more than two strides brought me in view of the door. The light being more dim, and my eyes just escaping from the foot-lights, I did not see so well, but I could see the door there and noticed this person. Of course I passed the person, and could easily have put my hand on him.

Q. Will you please mark on the plat or diagram, already shown you, the position in which you were when you saw that person? Put your initials on the plat at the spot, and indicate the position where that person stood?

The Witness marked with his initials on the diagram, which is Exhibit No. 48, the point supposed by him to be the door which was slammed, his own position at the time, and the position of the person near the door.

Q. Please mark also the positions of the other persons that you saw in the passage, as near as you can?

The witness marked the position as indicated by the question, and added:

I have made these marks as indicating, as near as I could from a judgement in such a rapid transit as I was making of the position of the persons I met.

Q. State as well as you can recollect whether the persons you saw there were gentlemen or ladies?

A. I think the majority of the persons that I observed were ladies.

Q. Did you notice Miss Laura Keene?

A. I did not, particularly; I should find it difficult to have noticed particularly any of the ladies, unless I had some means of knowing them, or had my attention called to them, any more than I knew that they were there, that they came out. All those persons, up to the point I described, were very much agitated, seemed very much confused. I saw another person to the right, or rather caught a glimpse of him, but that person was considerably in to the right of where the person was that I described as being near the door, and was moving.

Q. Moving which way?

A. In on the stage.

Q. Moving from the door?

A. He was moving almost at right angles to my course, off to my right.

Q. Was he moving away from the door, or getting nearer to the door?

A. He was moving away to the right, not moving away from a straight line with the door, but that person had not come from the door, or I would have seen him.

Q. You mean that as he moved he got further from the door?

A. Yes, sir; further from the door and further from me.

Q. Did you notice any person in the alley except the one who mounted and rode off?

A. As I passed out of the door, on the right side, a small person passed directly under my right elbow. I caught a glimpse of and rather felt the person. As I approached the horse at the nearest point—I got to the horse before he was sheared around from the right to the left—some one ran rapidly out of the alley.

Q. Was it probably the person you noticed passing at your elbow?

A. No, sir; that person never passed me; he was left behind me, wherever he went to.

Q. Could you recognize that person if you saw him.

A. No, sir; I could not. There was no light inside by which I could recognize him. The person, whoever it was, was a small person.

Q. Was he as tall a person as the prisoner Spangler?

A. No, sir; I should think not by four or five inches.

Q. Could you see whether the person who you now think was Spangler wore any whiskers or moustache at that time?

A. If he did it was not prominent, and I did not observe it so distinctly; and yet I am under the impression that his face was slightly bearded, but not to that prominent degree which would attract or fix, or settle my attention much. The visage was what I took in—the side face, the profile.

Q. Your impression is that his face was bearded?

A. Not prominently, I should have thought he had some beard on his face; but you can imagine if you associate your ideas with the attention I would be paying to any one who came near me, considering the object I was about, how this thing would strike me.

Q. Do you think he had a moustache only, or a moustache and side-whiskers?

A. I cannot undertake to say that there were any side-whiskers. I did not expect to be asked these questions, but I have always since then been under the certainty that I saw a person inside, near the door, and associating the appearance of that person, I have in my mind a certain profile, a certain visage, a certain appearance which rests in my conviction, and in my intelligence as to the person I saw.

Q. As to the moustache?

A. I am under the impression that there was some beard on the face, but I would not undertake to designate a moustache. If there was one it was not sufficiently prominent to make it marked in any way.

Q. Could you recollect how he was dressed?

A. No, sir.

Q. Could you recollect the color of any of his clothing?

A. I did not stop to take that particular notice. My recollection on that subject is that the person had on a grey or darkish suit. My recollection would be against its being a decidedly black suit.

Q. Have you seen the prisoner Spangler since then till now?

A. No, sir; I never saw him since then until to-day.

Q. And you swear, now simply to a mere impression, hardly a fixed opinion, as to his being the person?

A. I do not undertake to swear positively that that person sitting there was the person I saw. I do say that I saw a person there, and I see no person among these prisoners who calls to mind the appearance of that person except the one I have indicated, and that one, I am told, is Mr. Spangler.

Q. I wish to know how strongly you are of opinion, or under the impression, that that was probably the man, or whether you are under that impression?

A. I am decided in my opinion that the person now referred to resembles the person I saw there.

Q. I believe you returned to the theatre, after you chased Booth up the alley?

A. Yes, sir.

Q. You then came back to this door?

A. I entered the same door that I had gone out of.

Q. Do you not recollect meeting the prisoner Spangler as you came back?

A. If I did, I did not notice him in particular. When I got out from the door and from the time I reached the stage, I saw no one behind me, nor did I see any person after I passed beyond the door except the person on the horse whom I believed to be Mr. John Wilkes Booth, until I had run as far as I did run after the horse, which was around the alley and up to the left some little distance. I then turned and came back and saw that nobody had come out from the theatre up to that time. I asked some of the people in the buildings back if they had seen more than one horse there, and how long they had seen the horse there; and I got some answers from them which occupied but a moment and then went on into the theatre. One of the persons stated that he had seen one horse there and that was all they seemed to know. When I got inside the door again, I met four or five persons approaching the door, and just at the door one person, a policeman, a man with a police mark on and not this prisoner. Inside the door a number of persons came against me; the persons rapidly accumulated on my observation, returning into the house; the stage, the scenes, and the passage ways were all filling up.

Q. Do you recollect asking when you came in who that person was, or who it was that shot the President?

A. Oh, yes; I asked that question several times.

Q. Do you recollect this prisoner Spangler answering your question, saying it was Booth?

A. No, sir; I do not. I asked this question and recollect that one person answered it—"Are you satisfied it was Booth?"—"Have you any doubt it was Booth?" That was my belief, and I was rather eliciting the views of others. I would not undertake to say that he might not have been one of the persons who heard me ask the question, and, deeming it addressed to him, answered it; but I am not aware of addressing any question directly to that person.

Q. When you got out of the door, the person was just rising into his saddle, was he?

A. He was in his saddle, crouching forward, his left foot was in the stirrup; he was leaning to the left; the horse was moving with a quick sort of motion, making apparently more exertion than headway at that time, but still going pretty fast, and circling around. He was sufficiently mounted to go with the horse without being unbalanced; he

was getting the horse under control very fast for a forward movement.

Q. You cannot say, then, that he had just got into the saddle?

A. He was just completing his balancing himself in the saddle, but I should form the opinion from his position and the motion of the horse, that the moment he got his foot in one stirrup, he spurred the horse, and having the rein drawn more on one side than the other, for the moment lost control of him, so far as making him take a straight-forward movement.

By the JUDGE ADVOCATE:

Q. I understood you to say that all the persons you met in the passage as you approached that door exhibited signs of agitation, except this particular man?

A. Yes, sir, intense. Every person that came under my notice in the brief space of two seconds or three seconds that I ran through the stage, was greatly agitated and seemed literally bewildered. The only person that did not seem to be under the same state of excitement was the person who was near the door.

By Mr. EWING:

Q. How long did it take you, after you entered that passage, to get to the door?

A. I could hardly time myself.

Q. You were running?

A. Just as hard I could, and was only obstructed by the passing of those persons. Of course, it could not have been long; it could not have been five seconds from the time I got on that stage until I reached that door. It was very quick. I realized in my own mind something wrong immediately on hearing the report of the pistol. I knew there was no pistol fired in the play, and then the discharge of the pistol was overheard, and it was a charged pistol in my opinion. It was discharged either by accident or design, of course, and the design was solved by the circumstance of a man jumping out with a dagger in his hand, and the impression struck me instantly that there was something wrong. My impression was that that person coming from the President's box had assassinated or attempted to assassinate him. Every action which I performed, and every effort that I made after I started to get upon the stage, was acting under that conviction and impression to the last, so much so that I stated to the people in the tenement houses in the rear, before I returned, that the person who went off on that horse had shot the President.

Q. You saw only the side face of the person near the door?

A. A profile, but his full face passed around as you would see my own face now in turning from left to right.

By the JUDGE ADVOCATE:

Q. Did I understand you to recognize or to suppose you recognized Booth when he alit upon the stage?

A. Yes, sir. After I went out and returned, I took my family home, and immediately ran down the street toward Mr. Stanton's. I perceived persons in front of there and then turned and went rapidly to the police-station and gave my name and the information I had to Superintendent Richards, of the police, and upon his question, said to him that I believed I knew who it was that had committed the deed; that I believed it was Booth, and he said he believed so too.

Q. You had known him before by sight.

A. I had known him in this way: I had known him by sight, and I was some two years ago one evening at the Metropolitan Hotel introduced to him; I had seen him on the stage, and I had noticed him more during the last winter around the hotels. I went down two evenings to a hop at the National Hotel with some ladies, and I noticed him there leisurely around the parlor. I had not a doubt in my mind whom I was running after when I ran over the stage, and I should have been surprised to find it anybody else. I made every exertion to get through, and was astonished that the persons on the stage did not obstruct him, but they seemed very much bewildered. I felt a good deal vexed at his getting away, and had no doubt when I started on the stage that I could catch him.

By the Court:

Q. How long should you judge it to be from the time you heard the door slam until you saw the man balancing on his horse?

A. Not over the time in which I could make two steps.

Q. Were you nearer the door when you heard it slam than the horse was on which was the man?

A. That I cannot determine; for the horse was outside, and I was approaching the door through a passage-way that I had never been in before, and was only admonished of the position of the door by approaching it, and the slamming of the door indicated to me that there was a door, slammed right directly in front of the position I then occupied, and I am sure it could not have been over the second stride after that. As the light reflected back along the passage-way the door came in view, and this person that I have described was in the position described, and turning towards me from the door, and I suppose in three strides more I was at the door.

Q. Are you satisfied that the door was closed by some other person than the person who went out at the door?

A. I cannot possibly be satisfied of that at all. There is nothing to exclude from my mind the possibility of the door having been closed by the person who went out—by Booth himself—but I did not see him close the door. The first notice of the door was on my ear, and in a moment it was in view. At the same moment I perceived the person standing

as I have described, and the matter transpired then as I have stated, in my observation.

Q. Are you satisfied that the person you saw inside the door was in a position, and had the opportunity, if he had been disposed to do so, to have interrupted the exit of Booth?

A. Beyond all doubt.

Q. And from his manner he was cool enough to have done so?

A. He showed no agitation like the other people did.

By Mr. Ewing:

Q. Were not the other parties that you have spoken of also in a position to have interrupted the exit of Booth?

A. Yes, sir.

Q. All of them?

A. They were at the moment I saw them. They might have been two or three feet to the right or left in the scene-way before I saw them. Everybody I met could, if he had seen fit, have obstructed my motion; and if those persons occupied the same position when Booth went through, they could have obstructed his motion.

Q. That is all you meant to say?

A. One person only could not have obstructed my motion, and that was the person who was apparently three, four, or five feet off to the right. I could have passed out the door without his obstructing me. That is the person whom I described, who seemed to be passing off to the right. All the other persons I saw could, and in fact did, obstruct my motion by their presence, but made no physical effort.

Q. The person of whom you speak as being nearest to the door was in no better position to obstruct the movements of Booth, as far as you know, than any of the others?

A. None whatever, so far as I know.

Q. Was he not in a position which would be natural to a person who had run to see who it was passing out, and who, as the door slammed, turned?

A. Yes. A person who had made an effort to discover that object would occupy that position.

By the Court:

Q. This man was nearest of all, though, to the door?

A. Yes; nearest to the door.

Q. And could have opened it and gone out before you went out?

A. Oh, yes. It would have been but a step to the right, and a reach to open it; the door was immediately within the control of the person who stood there.

By Mr. Ewing:

Q. Do you know whether the persons you passed in the passage, any of them, knew that the assassination had been committed?

A. That would be but a conjecture. They acted more like people who were astounded at something that had just occurred without any means of knowing what their impressions were of the character of the occurrence; they were in that state of agitation.

MAY 23.

JOSEPH BURROUGH

recalled for the prosecution:

By Assistant Judge Advocate BINGHAM:

Q. State to the Court whether or not you were working at Ford's Theatre in January last.

A. Yes, sir; I was working there.

Q. State if you know the stable in the rear that was occupied by Booth with his horses and carriage.

A. Yes, sir.

Q. State if you know who fitted up that stable for Booth?

A. Spangler and a man by the name of George.

Q. What Spangler?

A. Ned Spangler.

Q. The prisoner here at the bar?

A. Yes, sir.

Q. Did he do that in January last, before Booth put the horses in it?

A. Yes, sir.

Q. What did he do to the stable?

A. He raised it up a little higher and put stalls in it.

Q. How many stalls did he put in it?

A. Two.

Q. Did he prepare a carriage room too?

A. Yes, sir; but first he had to raise it higher for the buggy.

Q. Was Booth there at the time when he was doing it?

A. He was there sometimes; he was there a little once.

Cross-examined by Mr. EWING:

Q. Did Booth occupy the stable with his buggy and horse?

A. Yes, sir.

Q. From that time on until the assassination?

A. Yes, sir. First he had a horse and saddle in there, and then he sold that horse and got a horse and buggy.

Q He had the horse and buggy there until the assassination?

A. Yes, sir.

By Assistant Judge Advocate BINGHAM:

Q. I would like to know what horse and buggy, if any, he sold before that time.

A. He sold the horse that he brought there first—the horse and saddle.

Q. Was there any buggy sold before that time?

A. No, sir; he sold the buggy last—the horse and buggy.

Q. When was it sold?

A. It was sold on Wednesday, I think.

Q. Was that the Wednesday before the President was murdered?

A. Yes, sir.

Q. Who sold it for him?

A. Spangler.

Q. What Spangler?

A. Ned Spangler.

Q. The prisoner here?

A. Yes, sir.

By Mr. EWING:

Q. Do you know to whom he sold it?

A. No, sir; I do not know who he sold it to. He brought it down to the bazaar on Maryland avenue, but could not get what he wanted for it, and then he sold it to a man who kept a livery stable, he said.

Q He took it down to the bazaar?

A. Yes, sir.

Q. Is that where they sell horses and carriages?

A. Yes, sir.

Q. Did you not go with Spangler when he went down to the bazaar?

A. Yes, sir; I went with him down to the bazaar.

Q. Did not Booth and Gifford tell Spangler on Monday to take it to the bazaar?

A. Yes, sir.

Q. And you cleaned it off?

A. Yes, sir; I went out there and cleaned it off.

By Assistant Judge Advocate BINGHAM:

Q. That was on the Monday before the murder, as I understand it?

A. Yes, sir.

JAMES L. MADDOX,

a witness called for the prosecution, being duly sworn, testified as follows:

By Assistant Judge Advocate BINGHAM:

Q. Were you employed in Ford's Theatre last winter?

A. Yes, sir; I was.

Q. State to the Court who rented the stable for Booth, which he occupied with his horse during the winter and on the night of the murder of President Lincoln?

A. I did.

Q. When did you rent that stable?

A. I think it was in December last.

Q. From whom did you rent it?

A. Mrs. Davis.

Q. For whom did you rent it?

A. For Mr. Booth.

Q. How was the rent paid to Mrs. Davis—monthly or quarterly?

A. Monthly.

Q. Who paid the rent?

A. I did.

Q. Who furnished the money?

A. Mr. Booth gave me the money.

Q. Were you present at the decoration of the President's box on Friday afternoon, the 14th of April last—the day of the President's murder?

A. I was there at one time.

Q. Do you know who decorated it?

A. I saw Harry Ford in there, decorating it.

Q. Did you see anybody else?

A. I do not recollect seeing any person else in the box. There may have been some person in there, but I did not see them.

Q. Do you know who put in that box, on that day, the rocking chair on which the President sat?

A. I do not; I saw the colored man Joe Simms with it on his head. He was coming down from up in Mr. Ford's room and going through the alley-way.

Q. He was bringing it into the theatre?

A. Yes, sir.

Q. Was that in the afternoon?

A. Yes, sir.

Q. Did you see who helped him to put it in that box?

A. No, sir.

Q. Had you ever seen that chair in that box at all?

A. Not this season.

Q. Had you ever seen it?

A. The first time the President ever came there it was put in there.

Q. When was that?

A. In the winter of 1863.

Q. Then you had not seen it there for two years?

A. No, sir.

Q. Were you in the box that day yourself?

A. No, sir.

Q. Had you been in the box a few days before?

A. No, sir; I have not been in that box since 1863.

Cross-examined by Mr. EWING:

Q. What has been your business at the theatre?

A. The property-man.

Q. Do your duties require you to be on the stage while the performance is going on?

A. Yes, sir; if there is anything to do. There is a great deal of work to do generally. Sometimes there is nothing at all, and I go out.

Q. What is your position on the stage?

A. To see that the furniture is put on there right; to give the actors any side-properties that are required to use in the piece.

Q. What place on the stage is yours—what part of the stage do you occupy?

A. My room is not on the stage; it is off the stage. I do not occupy any part of the stage particularly.

Q. You have no position on the stage?

A. No position on the stage proper.

Q. Do you know the passage-way by which Booth escaped?

A. I was shown the passage-way. I did not see him escape that way.

Q. Can you state whether it is customary during a performance to have that passage-way clear or obstructed?

A. It is generally clear. I have never seen it blocked up. When we are playing a heavy piece we generally have to run things in there in a hurry. It is generally clear.

Q. Is the "American Cousin" a heavy piece?

A. No, sir.

Q. Do you think, then, that during the play of the "American Cousin" that passage through which Booth passed would properly be clear, with no obstruction?

A. Yes, sir.

Q. Where was Spangler's position on the stage?

A. His position was on the left-hand side of the stage.

Q. The same side that the President's box was on?

A. Yes, sir; he has always been on that side since I have been about the theatre.

Q. Did you see Spangler that night?

A. Yes, sir, I did.

Q. State at what times you saw him, and where he was during the performance?

A. I saw him pretty nearly every scene. If he had not been there I should certainly have missed him, I do not recollect of seeing him away from the flats at all. He may have been away, but I cannot say.

Q. If he had been away you would have missed him?

A. Yes, sir; because some person would have had to run his flat off, and every person would have been inquiring where he was.

Q. If he had been away for what length of time?

A. If he had missed one scene we should have known it. Sometimes one scene lasts twenty minutes, and a man can go a good ways in that time.

Q. In the third act of the "American Cousin," are not the scenes shifted frequently?

A. Yes, sir; there are seven scenes in it, the way Miss Keene plays it.

Q. Would it have been practicable for Spangler to have been absent during the performance of that act?

A. No, sir, it would not; he ought not to have been absent.

Q. Would it have been practicable for him to be absent for five minutes, without his absence being noticed?

A. It would.

Q. Ten minutes?

A. No; even five minutes' absence would have been noticed during the third act.

Q. How was it during the second act?

A. I guess he has half an hour in the second act, and in the first scene of the third act he has twenty-five minutes. After the first scene of the third act he has twenty-five minutes. After the first scene of the third act, the scenes are pretty quick.

Q. Were you at the front of the theatre during that play?

A. During the second act I was in the box office.

Q. Were you on the pavement?

A. I went through the alley-way to the

front of the house. I had to go on the pavement.

Q. Did you see Spangler there?
A. I did not.

Q. Did you ever see Spangler wear a moustache?
A. Not since I have known him, and I have known him two years-next month.

Q. Where were you at the moment the President was assassinated?
A. I was in the first entrance, left hand.

Q. That is the side the President's box is on?
A. Yes, sir.

Q. Did you see Spangler very shortly before that?
A. Yes, sir; I think I did. I saw him standing at his wing when I crossed the stage with the will while the second scene of the third act was on.

Q. You saw him in his place then?
A. Yes, sir.

Q. How long was that before the President was assassinated?
A. I think that was about three or four minutes; it could not have been longer than that before, but I will not say positively.

Q. When you heard the pistol fired did you see Booth spring upon the stage?
A. No, sir.

Q. Did you see him run across the stage?
A. I first caught a glimpse of him when he was about two feet off the stage.

Q. Did you run after him?
A. I ran on the stage and I heard a call for water, and then I ran for water and brought a pitcher of water, and gave it to one of the officers.

Q. Did you see Spangler after that?
A. I did not see him after that until the next morning. I do not recollect seeing him at any rate. I may have seen him, but not have taken any notice of it.

Q. Did you hear Booth that night when he rode up to the theatre and called for Spangler?
A. I did not.

By Assistant Advocate BINGHAM:
Q. Do you know whether the President's box was locked, except when they were decorating it or when it was occupied?
A. I do not know. I am very seldom ever in the front of the house in the daytime.

Q. Do you know whether they were in the habit of keeping the outside door of it locked?
A. I do not.

Q. Do you whether any of the other boxes were occupied that night when the President sat in there?
A. I do not think any of them were.

Q. Do you not know they were not?
A. I do not. I cannot say positively whether they were or not.

Q. You do not think they were?
A. I do not think they were, but I would

not say positively they were not. I never took notice only first of the President's box, and saw that the President came in.

By Mr. EWING:
Q. When did you first hear that the President was coming to the theatre that night?
A. I heard it, I guess, about twelve o'clock.

Q. Who told you?
A. Mr. Harry Ford.

Q. Do you know whether the President was invited?
A. I do not. I heard that night that one of his young men, who were officers up there, came down and engaged the box for him. I heard him say so myself.

Q. Heard who say so?
A. I do not know what his name is, but he is one of the detectives up there at the President's House—a young man. I heard him say that night that he had come down that morning and engaged the box for the President.

JUNE 1.

JACOB RITTERSPAUGH

recalled for the prosecution.

By Assistant Judge Advocate BINGHAM:
Q. State to the Court whether you were a carpenter in Ford's Theatre down to the 14th of April last.
A. Yes, sir, I was.

Q. Were you there on the night of the 14th of April, when the President was shot?
A. I was.

Q. State which box in the theatre the President occupied that night.
A. It was on the left-hand side of the stage; on the right as you come in from the front.

Q. Did the President sit in the upper or lower box?
A. The upper.

Q. When the shot was fired did you hear anybody say anything about stopping a man?
A. Yes, sir.

Q. What was said?
A. Somebody hallooed, "Stop that man."

Q. State where you were at the time and what you did when you heard that cry "stop that man?"
A. I was standing on the stage behind the scenes. Some one cried that the President was shot. Then I saw a man running that had no hat on.

Q. Which way was he running?
A. Towards the back door. He had a knife in his hand, and I ran to stop him and ran through the last entrance, and as I came up to him he tore the door open. I made for him, and he struck at me with the knife, and I jumped back then. He then ran out and slammed the door shut. I then went to get the door open quick, and I thought it was a kind of fast; I could not get it open. In a

moment afterwards, I opened the door and the man had just got on his horse and was running down the alley; and then I came in. I came back on the stage where I had left Edward Spangler, and he hit me on the face with the back of his hand, and he said, "Don't say which way he went." I asked him what he meant by slapping me in the mouth, and he said "For God's sake, shut up," and that was the last he said.

Q. Is the Edward Spangler to whom you refer the prisoner at the bar?

A. Yes, sir.

Q. When you went out of that door, had anybody else except the man that ran with the knife gone out before you?

A. I did not see any one else.

Q. Did any go out after you?

A. Some one came out, but I do not know who it was.

Q. Did you leave the door open when you went out?

A. Yes, sir; I left it open.

Q. What do you do during the time the play is going on in the theatre, if anything?

A. My business is to shift wings on the stage and pull them off, and fetch things out of the cellar if they need anything.

Q. State what sort of a man, if any, came out after you had gone out of the door.

A. I thought it was a tall man and a pretty stout man.

Q. Do you know him?

A. No, I did not take notice who it was.

Q. When you came back into the theatre, was the door open or shut?

A. It was open.

By Mr. EWING:

Q. Where were you standing when you heard the pistol fired?

A. In the centre of the stage.

Q. Where was Spangler then?

A. He was at the same place, just about ready to shove off the scenes, and I was there and listening to the play.

Q. Which was nearest the door, you or Spangler?

A. I was.

Q. You are certain you both stood there together when the pistol was fired?

A. Yes, sir.

Q. When the pistol was fired, did you know what had happened?

A. Not right away. First some one hallooed, "Stop that man," and then after that some one said the President was shot, and it was only then that I knew what had happened.

Q. You did not know what had happened until the President was shot?

A. No, sir.

Q. When you came back, whereabout was Spangler?

A. At the place I left him; the same place.

Q. Was there a crowd in there then?

A. The actors were there, and some strangers.

Q. Who were there right by you?

A. There were some women standing there; I do not know who they were—some that belonged to the theatre, but I do not know their names.

Q. Do you not know one of them?

A. I do not know any of their names. I am not acquainted with them. I had been there only about four weeks.

Q. Did any one of them take part in the play that night?

A. Yes, sir, I think some did.

Q. What parts did those take who were standing there when Spangler slapped you?

A. The one they used to call Jenny was standing there then. I do not know what part she took.

Q. How close was she standing to you and Spangler when he struck you?

A. She might have been three or four feet from me.

Q. She probably heard him say that?

A. I do not know.

Q. He said it loud enough for her to hear?

A. He did not say it so very loud.

Q. He said it in the usual tone?

A. Yes; but he looked as if he was scared, and a kind of crying.

Q. Did you not hear the people then hallooing "burn the theatre?"

A. No, sir; I just heard them halloo "hang him" and "shoot him." That was all I heard.

Q. Did you afterwards tell to a number of persons what Spangler said to you when he slapped you?

A. Not that I know of. I think some detective came and asked something about the theatre, and I told him about Spangler hitting me in the mouth with his open hand.

Q. Did you not tell Mr. John T. Ford?

A. No, sir.

Q. Did you tell either of the Messrs. Ford?

A. No, sir. I never knew John T. Ford until I saw him after the thing had happened.

Q. Did you say nothing to any of the Fords about what Spangler had said to you when he slapped you?

A. I told it to nobody but Gifford, the boss.

Q. You told Gifford?

A. Yes.

Q. Where did you tell Gifford?

A. At the prison.

Q. What did you tell Gifford that Spangler had said?

A. I told him that Spangler said I should not say which way the man went.

Q. When was it that you told Gifford?

A. It was the same week I was released, I think.

Q. At Carroll Prison?

A. Yes, sir.

Q. How many weeks ago?

A. I think it was the week before last, if I am not mistaken.

Q. Did you tell anybody else that?

A. Not that I know of.

Q. To what detective did you tell it.

A. I do not know his name. It is the man that had me arrested.

Q. When did you tell it to him?

A. After I was released from the prison.

Q. Where did you tell him?

A. At the house where I board. He came up there the same day, I think; it was on Friday, I believe.

Q. How long was it after you were released?

A. In the afternoon; I was released at eleven o'clock, and in the afternoon he came there, about three or four o'clock.

Q. What kind of looking man was the detective?

A. He has black whiskers and moustache.

Q. How heavy a man?

A. About one hundred and forty pounds, I should think.

Q. How was he dressed?

A. In black. He is one of Colonel Baker's men.

Q. Do you know what they call that detective?

A. No; I do not know his name.

Q. You told it to nobody else, then, but to Gifford and that detective?

A. That is all, as far as I can remember.

Q. See if you cannot recollect somebody else to whom you told it?

A. I may have said something in the house at the table when I came in there: I think the rest of them heard it.

Q. Where were you?

A. At the boarding house where I generally board.

Q. Were you at a meal when he came in?

A. No; I think I was sitting in front of the house when he came.

Q. Did you see Booth open the back door of the theatre?

A. Yes, sir.

Q. Did you see him shut it?

A. Yes, sir; but I did not know who he was then; I did not see his face right.

Q. You were the next person who got to the door after he left?

A. Yes, sir.

Q. Then who opened it?

A. I opened it.

Q. Did you shut it?

A. No, sir.

Q. How close to you was the big man who ran out after you?

A. He might have been perhaps five or six yards from me when I heard him holla, "Which way?" I do not know, I cannot say for certain, whether it was he or some one else who hollaed "which way." I cried out

"this way," and then ran out and left the door open. By that time the man had got on the horse and gone off down the alley.

Q. Where did you see the big man again?

A. Outside.

Q. Have you seen that big man since?

A. No, sir; I did not take notice what kind of looking man he was.

Q. He is a good deal taller man than you are?

A. Yes, sir.

Q. Is he not considerably over six feet high?

A. I cannot say whether he was over six feet, but he was a tolerably tall man.

Q. How long was it after you went out before you came back to where Spangler was standing?

A. It might have been two or three minutes.

Q. And he was crying, you say?

A. He looked the same as if he was crying and a kind of scared.

Q. What did you say to him first before he said that to you?

A. I did not say anything to him.

Q. What else did you hear the people holla?

A. "Hang him," "Shoot him," was all I heard them holla. That was the last.

Q. Did you hear them call any names?

A. No, sir.

Q. Did any one call Booth's name?

A. Not that I know of.

Q. When did you find that it was Booth who had shot the pistol?

A. After the people were all out and I came outside. Some said it was Booth and some said it was not.

Q. It was after Spangler had slapped you?

A. Yes, sir.

Q. Did you hear them talk about burning the theatre?

A. No, sir.

Q. You and Spangler were standing where you were for the purpose of shifting the scenes?

A. It was not my place to shove them; my work is generally to pull off the things and shove them on.

Q. But that was Spangler's place?

A. Yes, sir; and some other man's, whose name I do not know.

Q. Spangler was there, then, where he ought to be to do the work that he had to do?

A. Yes, sir.

Q. How many persons were inside the theatre about the door when you came back?

A. I cannot tell how many; there were a good many. They were still running down from upstairs asking which way the man went, and I told them he had gone out the back way.

Q. That was after you saw Spangler the second time?

A. Yes, sir; that was afterwards.

Q. You are certain Booth opened the door himself and shut it, and that then you were the next person who opened it?

A. Yes, sir.

Q. And you left the door open?

A. Yes, sir.

Q. Were you at supper with Spangler that night?

A. Yes, sir.

Q. Before the assassination?

A. Yes, sir; we went home together at six o'clock and came back at seven.

Q. You boarded together?

A. Yes, sir.

H. CLAY FORD,

a witness called for the accused, Edward Spangler, being duly sworn, testified as follows:

By Mr. EWING:

Q. State what business you were engaged in on the 14th of April last, and immediately preceding.

A. Treasurer at Ford's Theatre.

Q. State when it was first known there that the President was going to the theatre that night.

A. It was first known to me about half after eleven o'clock. I had been to breakfast, and did not get back until some time after the President had engaged the box.

Q. State whether John Wilkes Booth was at the theatre after that on that day; and if so, at what time.

A. He was there, I think, about twelve o'clock noon, half an hour after I came to the theatre myself.

Q. State whether or not the fact that the President was going to the theatre that night was communicated to Booth

A. I do not know. I think very likely he found it out there. I am not certain whether he did or did not. I did not tell him. It might have been told there at the time that the President was coming.

Q. Did you see anything of Booth afterwards on that day?

A. No, sir; not until the evening.

Q. Did you see him as you were going to the theatre that day?

A. No, sir; I saw him coming down the street, I think, while I was standing in the door of the theatre.

Q. State what he did then.

A. He then went and commenced talking to the parties standing around. Mr. Raybold went into the house and brought him out a letter that was there for him; he sat down on the steps and commenced to read it.

Q. At what time was that he came there?

A. About twelve o'clock noon.

Q. How long did he stay?

A. I should think he stayed about half an hour; he conversed a while there and read the letter, and I went into the office; and when I came out again he had gone.

Q. State what you know about the preparation of the theatre for the reception of the President at that time.

A. When I went to the theatre, my brother, James R., told me the President was to be there that night, and I told Mr. Raybold about fixing up and decorating the box for the President that night. He had the neuralgia in his face, and I fixed it up in his place. I went up there and found two flags there ready to be put up, got Mr. Raybold to help me put up those two, and another flag came down from the Treasury Department. I went up there and put up the regimental colors, blue flag, in the centre, and above the two American flags. I had part of the furniture, one chair, brought from the stage and put in the box, and the sofa and a few chairs out of the reception room, and the rocking-chair down from my sleeping room up stairs, next door to the theatre.

Q. Did you receive any suggestion from anybody as to the preparation of the box?

A. Only from Mr. Raybold, and the gentleman who was there at the time that brought the third flag down from the Treasury building and helped me to decorate the box.

Q. What had Spangler to do with the decoration of the box?

A. He took the partition out of the box; there are two boxes, and taking out the partition makes them one?

Q. Was it usual to remove that partition upon any such occasion?

A. Yes, sir; we always removed it when the President came there.

Q. You had removed it when the President attended the theatre?

A. Yes, sir. Spangler and the other carpenter, Jake, removed it, I believe.

Q. How many times had the President been at your theatre during the spring and winter?

A. I do not know. I suppose about six times during spring and winter. He was there three or four times during Mr. Forrest's engagement, and twice during Mr. Clarke's engagement. Those are the only times I remember.

Q. How did Spangler come to the box? Was he sent for?

A. I suppose Mr. Raybold sent for him. I did not speak to him about taking out the partition from the box. I do not know myself.

Q. Was Spangler in the box during the time you were there decorating it?

A. No, sir. Spangler was on the stage at that time.

Q. What was he doing?

A. He was working on the stage. I think he had a pair of flats lying down on the surface of the stage, fixing them in some way. I called for a hammer and nails, and he threw up to me two or three nails and handed me the hammer up from the stage.

Q. Do you know whether he was apprised of the fact that the President was coming or not?

A. Oh yes, sir; he knew the President was coming, because he was taking out the partition.

Q. Do you know whether there was any penknife used in the decoration of the President's box, and what became of the pen-knife?

A. I used the penknife in cutting the strings to tie up the flags and the picture of Washington, and left it there in the box.

Q. You left it there?

A. Yes, sir.

Q. Did you forget it?

A. Yes, sir; I forgot it.

Q. Had the picture of Washington been there before?

A. No, sir.

Q. Why was the chair that was there brought from your sleeping room to the President's box?

A. Only because putting the other furniture in, I put the chair in with it, the chair belonged to the same set. The chair was in the reception room in the first place, and the ushers going in there and sitting in it greased it with their hair, and we had to remove it up to our room, being a very nice chair. We put the red furniture in the box that day, and we put in the chair because it belonged to that set—that was the only reason for putting it in—so as to make the box look as neat as possible.

Q. Do you know whether Booth was in the habit of engaging any of the boxes?

A. Yes, sir.

Q. What box was he in the habit of engaging?

A. The one he always engaged, when he engaged any, was box No. 7, on the right hand side of the theatre, the one nearest the audience; it is a part of the President's box when the partition is taken out.

Q. It was one of the boxes that the President occupied?

A. Yes, sir.

Q. How often did he occupy that box, during the season, before the assassination?

A. He secured the box three or four times; I do not know whether he ever occupied it or not; I never saw him in the box. He spoke to me of bringing some ladies, and sometimes he would use the box, and sometimes he would not.

Q. Did he ever occupy any other box?

A. Not to my knowledge.

Q. Do you know whether Booth's spur caught, as he leaped from the box, in anything; if so, in what?

A. I have heard that it was caught in the flag, but I do not know.

Q. In what flag?

A. I understood that it was the blue flag in the centre. I always understood so; I do not know it.

Q. Who put the flag on there?

A. I placed the flag there.

Q. That afternoon?

A. Yes, sir.

Q. Where did you get that flag?

A. It came from the Treasury Building—the Treasury regiment flag.

Q. Was there anything special or unusual in the arrangement of that box, and if so, what?

A. The picture had never been placed in front of the box before. We mostly always used small flags, but on this occasion, as General Grant was expected to come with the President that day, we borrowed these flags from the Treasury regiment to decorate it with.

Q. State where you were during the play of the "American Cousin," preceding the assassination.

A. I was in the ticket office of the theatre.

Q. Were you out on the pavement at all?

A. I may have been out on the pavement; I do not remember being there. I suppose I passed in and out two or three times.

Q. Did you see anything of the prisoner, Edward Spangler, in front of the theatre during the play?

A. No, sir.

Q. Did you ever see him wear a moustache?

A. No, sir.

Cross-examined by Assistant Judge Advocate BINGHAM:

Q. You know the fact, I suppose, that the other boxes of that theatre were not occupied on the night of the assassination?

A. Yes, sir. None of the boxes were occupied, I think. I could tell by looking at my book. I am not certain of it.

Q. Have you not had particular attention called to that matter since the assassination?

A. Yes, sir. I do not remember of any boxes being taken on that night.

Q. Do you not remember the further fact that the boxes were applied for that evening, and the applicants were refused, and told that they had already been taken?

A. No, I do not recollect it. The applicants did not apply to me.

Q. You sold all the tickets, did you not?

A. No, sir, there were four of us in the office who sold tickets.

Q. And you do not know who had applied for those other boxes?

A. No, sir.

Q. Are you willing to swear here that Booth did not?

A. To me? Yes, sir.

Q. To anybody, with your knowledge?

A. Yes, sir, I swear he did not.

Q. To you, according to your information?

A. According to my information, he did not.

Q. Nor anybody else for him?

A. Nor anybody else for him.

Q. There were no applications of any kind for the other boxes to your knowledge?

A. To my knowledge, no application was made for any box except the President's.

Q. I understand you to swear, however, that there may have been applications made, and you know nothing about them?

A. Yes, sir, there may have been.

Q. Now will you please tell the Court whether there was a mortise in the wall behind the entrance door of the President's box when you were up there decorating it?

A. I did not notice it.

Q. Will you swear whether there was or was not a mortise there?

A. There was not, to my knowledge.

Q. You know there was one there when the President was murdered?

A. I do not know it; I heard so.

Q. Did you not see it afterwards?

A. No, sir.

Q. You did not see it afterwards?

A. No, sir; I have not been in the box since.

Q. Was there any bar there for the purpose of fastening the entrance door of that box when you were there that afternoon?

A. I saw none.

Q. Was there ever such a contrivance attached to it before that day?

A. I never knew of any.

Q. Do you not know that there was a contrivance by which the door could be fastened at any time against its being opened from the outside by putting a bar in the mortise of the wall?

A. I know there was not.

Q. That is what I suppose—before that day?

A. Yes, sir.

Q. Was there a hole bored through the first door that opens into the President's box from the entrance passage before that day?

A. I never saw it, and do not know of any being there.

Q. Do you not know now that there is one there?

A. I have heard so, but I have not been in the box since.

Q. Have you not seen it since the assassination?

A. No, sir.

Q. Were the screws of the keepers of the locks of the doors to the President's box drawn before that day, so that the locks would not hold the door?

A. I have heard that the lock was bursted some time previous to the President's visit there; but I do not know about that.

Q. I am not asking you about any bursting. I am asking you about the fact whether the screws were drawn so that the keepers of the lock would not hold the door at all, if there was a pressure against it, opening into the President's box, before that day.

A. Not to my knowledge; I do not know.

Q. Do you swear that they were not so drawn when you were decorating the box that day?

A. To my knowledge, I swear they were not. They might have been drawn; I am not certain of that, but I did not notice it. I swear positively that I did not notice it.

Q. It was not done in your presence?

A. No, sir.

Q. Nor was it done with your knowledge?

A. No, sir.

Q. Had you a conversation with Mr. Ferguson before that about decorating the theatre with a flag in celebration of some of our victories?

A. I do not remember any.

Q. Or in regard to running up a flag on the theatre?

A. I do not remember ever having had any conversation with him on that subject; I may have had.

Q. Do you remember his asking you whether you had a flag to run up to celebrate a victory?

A. No, sir, I do not. I know that we borrowed a very large flag to run up in front of the theatre. My brother, James R. Ford, borrowed it.

By Mr. AIKEN:

Q. I understand you to state that it was half-past eleven or twelve o'clock when you first saw Booth in the theatre, in the morning?

A. It was about twelve o'clock, noon.

Q. How long did he remain there?

A. I suppose he remained there half an hour. I did not see him go. I stayed around there for about half an hour, I think, and then went into the office, and when I came out Booth had gone.

Q. Did Booth have this conversation and read this letter at that time?

A. Yes, sir.

Q. Did you see the letter?

A. Yes, sir.

Q. Was it a long or a short one?

A. It was a very long letter, either four or eight pages, either two sheets or one, I am not certain which, all covered over.

Q. Large size?

A. Yes, sir, letter paper.

Q. Had it been made public at the time Mr. Booth left the theatre that the President would be there that night?

A. When I came to the theatre my brother told me to wait there until he could go up and get the flags to decorate the box, and also to put a little notice in the Evening Star and the other evening papers of the President's visit.

Q. But the fact had not been made public then?

A. No, sir.

Q. Then could any one have had knowledge of that fact, unless they did come to the theatre?

A. Unless they met my brother, I do not think they could have had.

Q. In what direction did Booth go after he left the theatre?

A. I did not see him.

Q. Did you see him again between that time and 2 o'clock?

A. No, sir.

Q. Have you any means of knowing whether he was at the theatre again or not during that time?

A. No, sir.

Q. Did Booth seem to be in a hurry to complete this conversation, read the letter, and get away from the theatre?

A. No, sir.

Q. When he learned the fact that the President would be there that evening, did you notice any particular change in his manner or appearance?

A. No, sir, he appeared the same as ever. He sat on the step, opened his letter, and commenced to read it, looking up now and then and laughing.

By Assistant Judge Advocate BINGHAM:

Q. Booth knew at noon that the President was to be there that evening?

A. Yes, sir.

By Mr. AIKEN:

Q. At the time of his visit he learned that fact?

A. Yes, sir.

Q. Do you recollect the name of the messenger from the White House?

A. No, sir; I do not know his name.

Q. You think, then, that Booth could not have been at the theatre during that visit more than half an hour altogether in reading that letter, and this conversation and everything?

A. He might have been more; I am not positive. I think it was about half an hour, though, from the time he came until I found that he had gone. When he came I went and spoke to him and then went into the box office; and when I came out again, in about half an hour's time, he was gone.

Q. Did this conversation take place in the vestibule of the theatre?

A. No, sir; it was out in front of the gallery steps, the first door below the office door.

Q. On the sidewalk?

A. Yes, sir; on the pavement.

Q. Where was he when he read the letter?

A. He walked up and sat on the step of the main entrance door of the theatre, and read his letter.

Q. Do you know of your own knowledge who was with Booth at the time he got through reading the letter and went away?

A. There were men around there talking to him. Mr. Gifford was there, I think; and I think Mr. Evans and Mr. Grillot.

Q. Is Mr. Evans an attache of the theatre?

A. Yes, sir, an actor there.

By Assistant Judge Advocate BINGHAM:

Q. You say Booth knew at noon that the President was to be in that theatre that night?

A. Yes, sir.

Q. You did not tell him, and you do not know what he knew about it before?

A. No, sir.

By Mr. AIKEN:

Q. You said it would be impossible for any one to have known it before, unless they were from the Executive Mansion or had been at the theatre.

A. Some one may have been at the theatre, and gone off and reported it between half-past ten and twelve o'clock. I think it was about half past ten that the messenger came.

Q. The fact was not made known by parties and the newspapers until the evening?

A. No, sir, not until the Star came out.

By Mr. EWING:

Q. Do you think that if there had been a hole in the wall in the little passage between the President's box and the wall, say four or five inches one way and two inches the other that you would have noticed it that day?

A. No, sir; I would have noticed it if it had stood out from the door, but the door being thrown back against the wall I would not notice it. The door was open, thrown back against the wall, on that day. If it came from the outside I would not notice it. if it came inside I certainly would have noticed it.

Q. Is not that passage way pretty dark?

A. Yes, sir.

Q. Even when the door is open?

A. Yes, sir.

Q. Did you observe the side of the wall to the right as you went in?

A. No, sir, I took no particular notice of it.

Q. You might or might not have noticed it, then?

Yes, sir.

Q. If there had been an augur hole through the side of the door would you be likely to have seen that?

No, sir, I do not think I would.

Q. If one or both of the screws fastening the keeper of the lock of the door leading into the President's box had been loose, do you think you would have noticed that?

A. No, sir, I do not think I would have noticed that.

Q. Was the door leading into the President's box from that little passage open or shut when you went into the President's box?

A. It was open.

Q. Did it remain open?

A. Yes, sir; I left it open when I came out.

Q. Did you notice any paper pasted on the wall to the right of that little passage, as you entered it?

A. No, sir.

Q. Would you have been likely to notice it if it had been there?

A. I do not think I would.

By Mr. AIKEN:

Q. Were you acquainted with Mr. John H. Surratt?

A. No, sir.

Q. [Exhibiting to the witness the photograph of John H. Surratt] State if you ever saw a gentleman about the theatre resembling that picture.

A. I do not remember of any. I never saw that face that I know of; it is not familiar to me at all.

By Mr. EWING:

Q. Did you ever see the prisoner, Arnold, about the theatre?

A. No, sir.

Q. Or anywhere?

A. No, sir.

By Assistant Judge Advocate BINGHAM:

Q. You never saw him anywhere, in any place?

A. No, sir.

Q. You do not know him?

A. I do not know him.

By the COURT:

Q. Do you not know that the intended visit of the President to the theatre was published in the morning papers on the 14th of April?

A. No, sir. It was not published in the morning papers.

By Mr Cox:

Q. It was published in the Evening Star?

A. Yes, sir.

By the COURT:

Q. Did you state in the drinking saloon on Tenth street, during that day, that the President was to be there in the evening?

A. Yes, sir, I might have stated so.

Q. Then it was known before the Evening Star was published?

A. Yes, sir, around the vicinity of the theatre.

By Mr. Cox:

Q. Was it announced that General Grant was to attend the theatre in company with the President?

A. Yes, sir.

WILLIAM WITHERS, JR.

recalled for the accused, Edward Spangler.

By Mr. EWING:

Q. In your previous examination you were unable to state definitely whether or not the door leading into the alley from the passage was shut when Booth rushed out. Can you now state definitely whether it was or not?

A. Yes, sir, the door was shut.

Q. Do you recollect that fact distinctly?

A. Yes, sir. After he made the spring, after he gave me the cut and knocked me down to the first entrance, I got a side view of him, and I saw that he made a plunge

right at the door. The door was shut, but it opened very easily. I saw that distinctly. He made a rush at the knob of the door and out he went and pulled the door after him.

Q. He shut it after him?

A. Yes, sir; he swung it as he went out.

By Assistant Judge Advocate BINGHAM:

Q. It opened very easily when Booth went out?

A. It appeared so to me.

By Mr. AIKEN:

Q. Were you at the theatre at twelve o'clock on that day?

A. I cannot recollect. I think I had a rehearsal at ten o'clock on that day. There was not any music in the "American Cousin" that required my services, but I think I had a rehearsal with my whole orchestra for the song I had composed.

Q. Did you or not see Booth there during the day?

A. No, sir.

Q. You did not see him at all?

A. No, sir.

JAMES R. FORD,

a witness called for the accused, Edward Spangler, being duly sworn, testified as follows:

By Mr. EWING:

Q. State what business you were engaged in at the time of, and immediately preceding the assassination of the President.

A. I was business manager of Ford's Theatre.

Q. Will you state when you became apprised of the fact that the President intended to visit the theatre that night?

A. At half-past ten on Friday morning.

Q. How did you become apprised of the fact?

A. The young man from the President's house that generally came for the box came on that occasion.

Q. Do you know who he was?

A. I do not know his name.

Q. What business was he engaged in at the White House, do you know?

A. He was a runner. He had been to the theatre half a dozen times for the box. I do not know in what capacity you would call him.

Q. Had the President been previously invited to the theatre for that night?

A. No, sir.

Q. State whether on that day, and if so, how soon after you received this information, you saw John Wilkes Booth.

A. I saw John Wilkes Booth about half-past twelve on the same day—about two hours after I received the information.

Q. Where did you see him?

A. At the corner of Tenth and E streets.

Q. Where did he go?

A. He was going up E street, towards Eleventh street.

Q. Had he been at the theatre before?

A. He was coming from towards the theatre. I was coming from the Treasury building myself.

Q. Had you any knowledge of the President's intention to visit the theatre that night prior to the receipt of this message?

A. No, sir.

Q. Did you have anything to do with the decoration of the box that the President was to occupy, and if so, what?

A. No, sir; I had nothing to do with it.

Q. Did you not procure anything to decorate it with?

A. I procured the flags from the Treasury Department.

Q. Were you able to get all the flags that you wished for the decoration of the theatre?

A. No, sir, I was not. I wished to procure a thirty-six feet flag which Captain Jones could not procure for me, he said.

Q State whether, upon any occasion, you have had any conversation with Booth as to the purchase of lands, and if so, where?

Assistant Judge Advocate BINGHAM. I object to the question.

Mr. EWING. Testimony has already been admitted on that point.

Assistant Judge Advocate BINGHAM. I know, but it is unimportant as to this man. There is no question about this man in the case.

Mr. EWING. It is very important as to one of the prisoners.

Assistant Judge Advocate BINGHAM. It cannot be important. This man cannot be evidence for any human being on that subject no matter what Booth said to him about it. I object to it on the ground that it is entirely incompetent, and has nothing in the world to do with the case. But if this witness had been involved in it, I admit it might be asked with a view to exculpate him from any censure before the public

Mr. EWING. The Court will recollect that in Mr. Weichmann's testimony there was evidence introduced by the prosecution of an alleged interview between Dr. Mudd and Booth at the National Hotel, in the middle of January, which was introduced as a circumstance showing his connection with the conspiracy, which Booth is supposed to have then had on foot. The accused, Dr. Mudd, is represented to have stated that the conversation related to the purchase of his lands in Maryland. I wish to show by this witness that Booth spoke to him frequently, through the course of the winter, of his speculations —of his former speculations in oil lands, which are shown to have been actual speculations of the year before—and of his contemplating the investment of money in cheap lands in lower Maryland. The effect of the testimony is to show that the statement, which has been introduced against the accused, Dr. Mudd, if it was made, was a bona

fide statement, and related to an actual pending offer, or talk about the sale of his farm to Booth.

Assistant Judge Advocate BINGHAM. The only way, if the Court please, in which they can do anything in regard to this matter of the declaration of Mudd, if it was made, (and, if it was not made, of course it does not concern anybody,) is simply to show by legitimate evidence that there was such a negotiation going on between himself and Booth. The point I make is, that it is not legitimate evidence, or any evidence at all, to introduce a conversation between Booth and this witness at another time and place, It is no evidence at all, it is not colorable evidence and the Court have nothing in the world to do with it. It is utterly impossible to ask the witness any conceivable question that would be more irrelevant or incompetent than the question that is now asked him.

Mr. EWING. I will state to the Court further that it has already received testimony, as explanatory of the presence of Booth in Charles County, of his avowed object in going there—testimony to which the Judge Advocate made no objection, and which he must have then regarded as relevant. This testimony is clearly to that point of explanation of Booth's visit in lower Maryland, as well as an explanation of the alleged conversation with Mudd in January.

Assistant Judge Advocate BINGHAM. The difference is this: the defence attempted to prove negotiations in Charles county, and we thought we would not object to that; but this is another thing altogether. It is an attempt to prove a talk irrespective of time or place, or anything else.

The COMMISSION sustained the objection.

By Mr. EWING:

Q. Do you know anything of the visit made by Booth into Charles county, last fall?

A. He told me ——

Assistant Judge Advocate BINGHAM objected to the witness giving the declarations of Booth.

The WITNESS. I have never known Booth to go there.

Q. [By Mr. EWING.] Have you ever heard Booth say what the purpose of any visit which he may have made last fall to Charles county was?

Assistant Judge Advocate BINGHAM renewed his objection.

The COMMISSION sustained the object.

Q. [By Mr. EWING.] Do you know John McCullough, the actor?

A. Yes, sir.

Q. Do you know whether or not he was in the city of Washington on the 2d of April last.

A. I do not.

Q. Do you know where he was then?

A. No, sir.

By Mr. Cox:

4

Q. Did you send a notice of the President's intended visit that evening to the theatre to the Evening Star?

A. Yes, sir.

Q. Do you remember whether that notice announced that General Grant was to be there with him?

A. Yes, sir.

By Mr. AIKEN:

Q. At what time in the afternoon did you send that notice?

A. I sent it about twelve o'clock in the morning, as near as I can recollect.

By Assistant Judge Advocate BURNETT:

Q. In whose handwriting was that notice?

A. In my handwriting.

Q. Did you write it?

A. Yes, sir.

Q. About what time did the edition containing that notice first appear?

A. About two o'clock, I should think.

By Mr. AIKEN:

Q. I understand you to say that you sent that notice to the Star office before you met Booth coming up E street towards Eleventh?

A. Yes, sir.

Q. Was any one in company with Booth?

A. No, sir.

Q. Did you have any conversation with Booth that day?

A. I had no conversation with him; I merely spoke to him and asked—

Assistant Judge Advocate BINGHAM. You need not state anything about it.

Q. [By Mr. AIKEN.] Did you know John H. Surratt?

A. No, sir.

Q. [Exhibiting to the witness a photograph of John H. Surrat.] Did you see a person of that description about the theatre that day?

A. No, sir; I never remember seeing him.

Q. At what thime did John McCollough, the actor, leave the city?

A. He left when Mr. Forrest left. I believe that was the fourth week of January.

Q. Was he to play an engagement with him?

A. Yes, sir.

Q. Did Mr. McCollough return to this city in company with Mr. Forrest, on the 1st of March?

A. He did, on Mr. Forrest's last engagement. I do not know what time that was.

Q. Was it before the 1st of April?

A. I think it was.

Q. On what night was it that they played the "Apostate?"

A. It was on Saturday night.

Q. Do you know of your own knowledge whether McCollough had left the city or not before the first of April?

A. I do not.

Q. What time did Mr. Forrest leave?

A. I do not recollect the time of his last engagement, but he left after his engagement was over.

Q. Have you the means at the theatre of verifying the facts as to when Mr. Forrest and Mr. McCullough did leave?

A. I have no means of verifying when Mr. Forrest left.

By Assistant Judge Advocate BURNETT:

Q. Where did you write that notice? Where were you when you wrote it?

A. In the office.

Q. In the office that you ordinarily occupy?

A. Yes, sir; the ticket office of the theatre.

Q. Who was present?

A. There was no one present when I wrote that.

Q. Had you any consultation with any one about sending the notice to the papers?

A. I spoke to Mr. Phillips about it.

Q. Who is Mr. Phillips?

A. Mr. Phillips was an actor in our establishment.

Q. Did you speak to him first about it?

A. I asked him to write me the notice.

Q. Did he write the notice or decline?

A. He said he would after he had done writing the regular advertisement. He was on the stage at the time.

Q. Did you speak to any one else about it, or did any one speak to you?

A. I spoke to my younger brother about the propriety of writing it.

Q. Did you speak to any one else?

A. No, sir; not that I remember.

Q. Had you seen Booth previous to the writing of that notice?

A. No, sir.

Q. At what time did you write the notice?

A. Between half-past eleven and twelve o'clock, I should judge.

Q. Did you send it immediately to the office after writing it?

A. I sent one to the Star immediately, and carried the other one to the National Republican myself.

J. L. DEBONAY,

a witness called for the accused, Edward Spangler, being duly sworn, testified as follows:

By Mr. EWING:

Q. State where you were on the night of the 14th of April.

A. I was at Mr. Ford's Theatre.

Q. What business were you engaged in there?

A. I was playing what is called "responsible utility" in the theatre.

Q. State whether you knew of Booth's having rode up to the alley door and called for Spangler.

A. Yes, sir; he came to the alley door and called for Spangler; he called me first; but whether he came on a horse or not, I do not know. He said to me, "Tell Spangler to come to the door and hold my horse;" I did not see a horse, though.

Q. What did you do?

A. I went over to where Mr. Spangler was, on the left-hand side, at his post, and called him from his post. Said I, "Mr. Booth wants you to hold his horse." He then went to the door, went outside, and was there about a minute, and Mr. Booth came in. He asked me if he could get across the stage. I told him no, the dairy scene was on, and that he would have to go under the stage, and co e up on the other side. About the time that he got upon the other side, Spangler called to me, "Tell Peanut John to come here and hold this horse; I have not time; Mr. Gifford is out in front of the theatre and all the responsibility of the scenes lies on me." I went on the other side and called John, and John went there and held the horse, and Spangler came in and returned to his post again.

Q. Did you see Spangler any more that evening?

A. I did, three or four times that evening.

Q. Where?

A. On the stage.

Q. In his proper position?

A. Yes, sir.

Q. At what times during the play?

A. I could not say for certain what times. It was between and during the acts.

Q. Did you see him about the time the shot was fired?

A. I saw him about two minutes before that, I think.

Q. Where was he then?

A. He was on the same side I was on—the same side as the President's box.

Q. Did you see him after the shot was fired?

A. Yes, sir; about five minutes afterwards.

Q. Where?

A. Standing on the stage with a crowd of people. There was a big crowd collected on the stage then.

Q. What was he doing then?

A. I did not take any notice of him at all.

Q. Did you see Booth as he left?

A. I saw him when he made his exit. I was standing in the first entrance, left-hand side. When he came to the centre of the stage I saw that he had a long knife in his hand. It seemed to me to be a double-edged knife, and looked like a new one. He paused about a second, I should think, and then went off, the first entrance right-hand side.

Q. Did you see anybody follow him soon?

A. I think he had time to get out the back door before any person was on the stage.

Assistant Judge Advocate BINGHAM. You need not state what you think; state what you saw.

The WITNESS. I did not see the man get on the stage until he made his exit.

Q. How long was it after he made his exit that you saw any man get on the stage?

A. I cannot say exactly; I should say about two or three seconds.

Q. After he had passed out?

A. After he had got off the stage.

Q. Who got on the stage first after Booth left?

A. A tall, stout gentleman with gray clothes on. I think he had a moustache; I am not certain.

Q. What did he do?

A. He made the exit the same way Mr. Booth did.

Q. Do you think Booth had time to get out of the theatre before this other man got on the stage?

A. I cannot say for certain.

Q. State what you think about it.

Assistant Judge Advocate BINGHAM objected to the question, and it was waived.

By Mr. EWING:

Q. How rapidly did Booth move as he passed out?

A. He did not seem to run very fast. He seemed to be kind of stooping a little when he ran off.

Q. Do you know the distance to the door leading into the alley?

A. From the "prompt place" to the door, I think, is about forty feet, I should say—very near, between thirty-five and forty feet.

Q. How long do you think it was after he went out the first entrance before this man got on the stage?

A. I said about two or three seconds; I think it was about two or three seconds. I will not be certain about it. I think it was two or three seconds, though. I know he was out of my sight before this gentleman was on the stage.

Q. Do you think it was or was not long enough for Booth, moving at the rate he was going when you saw him, to get out of the back door before this man got upon the stage?

A. I do not know.

Q. How long was it before this large man who jumped upon the stage followed Booth?

A. I do not know whether he followed him or not. He went out the same way Booth did.

Q. How long was it after Booth went out before he went out?

A. About two or three seconds.

Q. Was he running faster than Booth, or not?

A. He did not seem to run very fast. Between the speed of the two, I think Booth was running the fastest.

Q. By Mr. AIKEN:

Q. Where were you at 12 o'clock in the day on Friday, the 14th of April last?

A. I think I was at the theatre, I am very sure I was; because there was a rehearsal there—a rehearsal of "American Cousin."

Q. Do you know J. Wilkes Booth, the actor?

A. Yes, sir.

Q. Did you see him there at that time?

A. I did not.

JAMES J. GIFFORD,

recalled for the accused, Edward Spangler.

By Mr. EWING:

Q. Do you know anything of a horse and buggy belonging to Booth having been sold a week or so before the assassination?

A. I heard Mr. Booth tell Mr. Spangler to sell the horse and buggy on Monday evening, one week previous to the assassination—to take it down the Tattersall and sell it.

Q. The Tattersall is a horse market in the city?

A. Yes, sir.

Q. Who sold the horse and buggy?

A. Mr. Spangler, I presume.

Q. Who received the money from the sale?

A. Mr. Spangler brought the man up with him, and asked me to count the money and give him a receipt. Mr. Richard Ford wrote the receipt; I took the money and handed it over to Booth.

Q. Do you know Jacob Ritterspaugh, who was a witness called yesterday?

A. I know a man that works at the theatre of that name; I am not much acquainted with him. He was only there some four weeks.

Q. State whether or not, since the assassination and previous to his release from Carroll prison, he told you at the prison that the prisoner, Edward Spangler, directly after the assassination of the President in the theatre, hit him in the face with the back of his hand and said, "Don't say which way he went."

A. To the best of my knowledge, I never heard him say so. He asked me if he could amend the statement that he had made. He said he had not told all he knew, and he asked me if he could amend it. I told him certainly, but he ought to be particular and state the truth of what he knew. That is all the conversation we ever had regarding it. He told me he had made a misstatement, and had not told all he knew.

Q. Did he say what he had omitted?

A. No, sir.

Q. Did he say that Spangler had slapped him on the face?

A. No, sir; not to me.

Q. Did he say that Spangler had said, "Don't say which way he went?"

A. No, sir, not to my knowledge.

Q Did he say anything to that effect?

A. No, sir, nothing of that kind at all to me.

Q. If he had said it you would likely have recollected it?

A. I should recollect it, I think, from the short time that has elapsed, and my mind being placed on the thing altogether. I have had nothing else to think about but this case since I have been in the Old Capitol.

Q. You think you certainly would have recollected it if he had told you?

A. I think so. He seemed in a great deal of trouble about not making a full statement, and he asked me about it, and I told him certainly they would allow him to correct anything he had done wrong.

Q. Did he make any allusion to the points that he had omitted?

A. No, sir, he did not—not to me.

Q. State whose business it was at Ford's Theatre to see that the locks on the doors in and about the private boxes, if they became broken, were repaired.

A. It was the business of the usher to inform me of the fact, and for me to have them repaired.

Q. State whether within your knowledge or information any repairing was done to any lock on the door leading into the box which the President occupied within six weeks or two months previous to the assassination.

A. None to my knowledge since the lock has been put on.

Q. When was the lock put on?

A. We opened about August, and it was about the latter part of August or the first of September of the year before last.

Q. State whether you know anything of the accused, Edward Spangler, being accustomed to crabbing and other fishing during the recesses of his engagement.

A. I never saw him at it; but I have known him to tell me that he went crabbing—that he would go down to the Neck on Saturday night, and stay until Monday morning, and come home on Monday morning. I have never seen him at it myself; but I know that is what he told me, and I have seen others who said the same thing—that they had been crabbing together.

Q. [Exhibiting to the witness the rope.] Will you state whether that rope is such a one as might be used in that sport?

A. They have a line something of this sort, and small lines tied on to it about that distance, [three feet,] with pieces of meat attached, and as they go along they trail it along. I have seen them at it, although I have never done anything at it myself. They pull up the crabs as they go along, and let the line go down, and dip them up out of the boat.

Q. They have short lines attached to the long one?

A. Yes, sir; short ones attached about three feet apart. That is the way I have seen them.

Q. With hooks and bait?

A. Yes, sir; there is just a string on it, and the meat is tied to the end of the string; the crab catches the end and they hook them on, and raise this line and get the crab from under it.

Q. Have you seen such ropes as that used in this sport?

A. Yes, sir, I have seen some similar, and some sometimes a little larger. It is not particular about the size. There is no strain on the rope.

By Assistant Judge Advocate BURNETT:

Q. At the places where they go crab-fishing they have lines there, have they not?

A. Sometimes they have on the shore, and sometimes persons carry them with them.

Q. There have to be little lines attached to the large line?

A. Yes, sir.

Q. And it requires considerable work to get the line into shape?

A. Yes, sir; they have to take and stretch it all out and play it over the shore, and straighten it all out.

Q. They usually have them ready made?

A. Sometimes the people on the shore have them, and sometimes people going from Baltimore take them with them.

Q. That rope is not ready for doing any fishing now, is it?

A. No, sir, it is not in condition.

By Mr. AIKEN:

Q. Were you at the theatre at 12 o'clock on Friday, the 14th of April, when J. Wilkes Booth came there?

A. I saw Mr. Booth pass between half-past eleven and twelve o'clock. I do not know exactly the moment.

Q. Did you have any conversation with him?

A. No, sir. I saw him go past the stage entrance and go to the front door. He bowed to me, but I did not have any conversation with him.

Q. Were you standing on the sidewalk at that time?

A. No, sir; I was standing in the alley gate, the entrance to the theatre.

Q. Who else was there at that time?

A. I think one of the Mr. Ford's was at the front door. I am not certain, perhaps both of them.

Q. Was Mr. Evans there?

A. I did not see him.

Q. Was Mr. Grillot there?

A. He might have been standing in his door for all I know. I did not see him. I was standing inside the alley gate.

Q. Did you hear any of the conversation going on at that time, if any, between Booth and the party with him?

A. No, sir; I heard none at all. He came up by himself.

Q. Do you what time it was that John McCullough left the city last?

A. No, sir; I could not tell you.

Q. Have you any means of finding out?

A. I could tell you the last night he played if I was at the theatre, but I cannot tell you what time he left the city.

Cross-examined by Assistant Judge Advocate BINGHAM:

Q. You say that Jacob told you he was greatly troubled because he had not made a full statement, and wanted to correct it?

A. He told me he was scared before; that he could not tell what he was doing, and he asked me if he could not make a correct statement, and I told him certainly.

Q. Did you not also state a minute ago that he seemed to be in great trouble?

A. He seemed to be troubled about it.

Q. How long ago was that?

A. I should judge it was about three weeks ago.

Q. He was in prison, was he not?

A. Yes, sir.

Q. It was long before he testified here the other day.

Yes, sir.

Q. Is it more than three weeks since Jacob made that statement to you?

A. It is fully three weeks.

Q. It is not four weeks?

A. I do not know I am not certain of the time.

Q. Do you remember his exact words when he made the statement?

A. He said he was scared so bad that he did not know what he was saying.

Q. What other words did he use?

A. I do not recollect—commonplace words.

Q. Did you not swear a little while ago that he said he had not told all he knew?

A. Yes, sir, I told you that.

Q. I know you told me that; but you do not seem to remember it.

A. I thought you asked me for something else.

Q. Now I want to know if you remember all the other words that he made use of when he made that statement?

A. No, sir, I do not.

JUNE 2.

CHARLES A. BOIGI,

a witness called for the accused, Edward Spangler, being duly sworn, testified as follows:

By Mr. EWING:

Q. State whether you know the accused, Edward Spangler.

A. Yes, sir, I know him; he has boarded at the same place I board at.

Q. How long before the assassination did he board at the place you were boarding at?

A. I do not know; it has been a good while; five or six months I presume.

Q. State whether or not he continued to board there after the assassination until his arrest.

A. He did.

Q. Did you see him at and about the house after the assassination, as usual?

A. Yes, sir; just as usual.

Q. Do you recollect the day of his final arrest?

A. No, sir, I do not.

Q. How long was it after the assassination before he was imprisoned?

A. They had him once or twice in the station-house, I believe. I do not recollect the date.

Q. But it was some days after the assassination before he left the boarding house, was it not?

A. Yes, sir.

JOHN GOENTHER,

a witness called for the accused, Edward Spangler, being duly sworn, testified as follows:

By Mr. EWING:

Q. Are you acquainted with the accused, Edward Spangler?

A. Yes, sir, I am.

Q. State whether or not you boarded with him previous to his arrest.

A. He boarded in the same house.

Q. How long had you boarded with him there?

A. I have boarded there, off and on, the last three years

Q. How long has he boarded there?

A. To my certain knowledge, he has boarded there, off and on, for six or seven months, if not longer. I am not certain as to the time.

Q. State whether or not, after the assassination, and up to the time of his arrest, you saw him about the boarding house as usual.

A. To my certain knowledge, I saw him, some two or three days after the assassination, about the house. I will not be very certain about the time; but I think I saw him for two or three days.

Q. Did you ever see him wear a moustache?

A. No, sir.

Cross-examined by Assistant Judge Advocate BINGHAM:

Q. What time of day did you see him about the house?

A. I saw him in the mornings and evenings, as I came from work. I work here in the arsenal, and generally take my dinner with me.

Q. What days of the week did you see him?

A. I am not certain what days they were.

Q. He did not sleep at that house?

A. No, sir.

THOMAS J. RAYBOLD,

a witness called for the accused, Edward Spangler, being duly sworn, testified as follows:

By Mr. EWING:

Q. How long have you lived in Washington, and what has latterly been your employment here?

A. I have not lived permanently in Washington. On the first Monday of December one year ago—the day Congress went in session—I recollect it well—I came to Wash

ington for Mr. Ford. I was employed there rather to take charge of the house, see to all the front of the house, purchased everything that was purchased for the house. If the repair of anything was needed in the front of the house, it was done through my order. That was my business there, and in the absence of the Messrs. Ford, I was in the box office at the theatre—sold the tickets.

Q. State whether or not you know anything of any portion of the locks on the private boxes being broken; and if so, state what you know.

A. I think it was during Mrs. Bowers's engagement in March—about the 7th—Mr. Merrick, of the National Hotel, while I was at dinner that day, asked me to reserve him some seats in the orchestra for some company that night—three, I think. I did so. He did not come up to the time the first act was over. It is customary, after the first act is over, for reserved seats which have not been occupied to be taken by any persons there wanting seats. That has been the general rule. He did not come up to the end of the first act, and those seats were occupied after the curtain fell at the end of the first act. Shortly after that he came in with his wife, Mr. Bunker's wife, and a gentleman from New York, with a lady. They sent to me in the front office, saying that Mr. Merrick was there and inquiring what did I do with those seats. I went in and saw that the usher had filled them. I then took him up stairs to a private box—box No. 6—but it was locked and I could not get in it. I crossed over the lobby again to boxes 7 and 8, generally termed the President's box, and they were also locked. The house was pretty well filled, and, on going back, I could not find the keys. I had not the keys with me, and could not find where they were. I supposed the usher had them, because he has frequently left the theatre after the first act. I put my shoulder against the door to force the door open. It did not give to that, and I raised and put my foot against it and gave it two or three kicks, and then it came open. That was the door to box 8, which is termed the President's box. I kicked that lock open on the evening of the 7th of March. There is another lock in the house to which I did the same thing when I could not find the key.

Q. State whether that door led into the box which the President occupied at the time of the assassination.

A. It did. That door led into the boxes which the President occupied—7 and 8. Both doors led into the box. When he occupied it both 7 and 8 were thrown into one box by taking down the partition between them. On no other occasions was that done, except by request. Then by request we would take out the partition and throw the box into one.

Q. When the two boxes were thrown together into one, which door was used to enter the double box?

A. Always the door to No. 8—the one I burst open.

Q. Do you know whether that was the door which was used on the night of the assassination?

A. It was; the other one could not be used.

Q. Do you know whether the lock was repaired after having been burst open?

A. I do not. I never examined it afterwards. I suppose it would have been my place to report it; but I never paid any attention at all to it afterwards—never thought of it, in fact, after that night. I frequently entered the box afterwards; always passed in without a key into the box, and never thought of having the lock fixed.

Q. To whom would you have reported it for repairs?

A. To Mr. Gifford.

Q. And you made no report of it to him?

A. No, sir; I never said anything about that—never thought of it—in fact, never thought it worth while mentioning it.

Q. State whether the locks were of any use?

A. The locks were but used to keep persons out when the boxes were not engaged. I have had frequently to go and order persons out of the boxes when they were left open. That was merely why the locks were used. After persons entered the box this door was mostly always left open. I have known it on several occasions to be left open.

Q. Can you say whether the door was locked at the time you burst it open?

A. Yes, sir: I know it was locked. I tried the door and could not open it. I forced with my shoulder against it. It was securely fastened. I stood from it with my back, and put my foot against it, right close to the lock, and the door flew open. I never examined it after I did that to know what condition it was in. I never thought of it afterwards to examine it.

Q. But you frequently entered the box afterwards?

A. I did on two or three occasions afterwards enter it, I know.

Q. And found no difficulty in entering it?

A. No difficulty at all.

Q. No necessity for using a key?

A. No. sir; there was no necessity for me to use a key after that: at least, I never took one with me. The keys generally were in the office during the day. During the night they were in possession of the usher.

Q. State whether you have any knowledge of Booth having occupied either of those boxes shortly before the assassination?

A. I cannot say precisely the time, but I think it was about two weeks prior to the 14th of April that Mr. J. Wilkes Booth engaged the private box No. 4, and came to the office again in the afternoon; I was sitting in the vestibule at the time, and asked for an exchange of the box. I think the exchange was made and he took box No 7, one of the boxes used for the President. That is the one in the door of which the hole was bored. I think Booth occupied that night box 7; but I cannot positively say it was that box, but I think it was. I know it was one of the two, either 7 or 8; but I cannot swear positively whether it was box 7 or box 8.

Q. It is the door leading into box 7 that has the hole bored throught it?

A. Yes, sir.

Q. State whether there were any box-tickets sold at the theatre up to the time of the opening on the night of the assassination.

A. To the best of my knowledge, there were not. I cannot say positively, for I do not know; but I know I sold none. I was not all the time in the office. I had been sick for three days with neuralgia, which I suffered from frequently, and I was not in the office all the time that day; but I was in the office during that afternoon, and I was there also in the morning when the tickets were obtained for the President by his messenger, but I do not know whether there were any sold, nor whether there were any applications made for them. Mr. Sessford is the best one to tell that; he knows it, I suppose.

Q. Would you have been likely to know if any of the tickets were sold?

A. Yes, sir; I would have seen in counting the house at night. I counted the tickets at the usual time, ten o'clock, on the night of the assassination.

Q. And you have no recollection of any of the box tickets having been sold?

A. No recollection of it.

Q. State at what hour the President engaged the seats?

A. Between ten and eleven o'clock in the forenoon, I think.

Q. Had he been previously invited?

A. Not to my knowledge.

Q. Did you see the messenger?.

A. I did, and was talking to him.

Q. State whether you saw anything of Booth that morning, after the President engaged the box?

A. I cannot say whether it was after the President engaged the box. or before it; but I saw him that morning. He got a letter from out of the office that morning; but I cannot say whether it was after the President's messenger was there, or prior to that. I know he got a letter. He generally came there every morning. His letters were directed to Mr. Ford's box in the Post Office, and when Mr. Ford came from breakfast in the morning, he would bring all the letters there, and what belonged to the stage would be sent back, and his would be called for by him.

Q. Did Booth get more than one letter that morning?

A. Not to my knowledge.

Q. State if you know any reason why the rocking-chair in which the President is said to have sat that night should have been in the position it was in.

A. I placed it in the position it was in on two or other occasions when the President occupied that box, simply because, if it had been in any other position in the box, the rockers would have been in the way. When the partition was taken down it left a triangular corner, and the rockers went into that corner, at the left of the balustrade of the box. The rockers went into that corner, and were out of the way. I cannot say what other purpose there was; that was the only reason why I put it there. I put it there on two occasions when the President was there, or, at least, had it put there myself.

Q. When was that?

A. Last season, while Mr. Hackett was playing.

By Assistant Judge Advocate BINGHAM:

Q. You mean last winter a year ago?

A. Yes, sir. It had not been used in there this last season up to this time, although the sofa and the other parts of the furniture had been.

By Mr. EWING:

Q. State what you saw of Spangler, if anything, for several days after the assassination?

A. I never saw him after the assassination, or; at least, I cannot recollect seeing him afterwards. I only know that he was arrested in the house on Saturday morning, the morning afterwards, but I did not see him, to the best of my knowledge.

Q. Was he not about the theatre that morning?

A. I cannot say. I do not know. I went home to Baltimore myself, where my family reside, on Saturday night. I have always been in the habit of going there on Saturday night or Sunday morning.

Q. When did you return?

A. I returned again on Monday morning.

Q. The theatre was shut up when you returned?

A. It was.

Q. [Exhibiting to the witness the coil of rope found in Spangler's carpet bag.] Look at this rope and state whether you know of such ropes being used about the theatre?

A. Yes, sir. I cannot swear that this is the rope, but we use such ropes as this. We used such ropes as this at the time of the Treasury Guard's ball to stretch from the lobby to the wings to hang on it the colors of different nations. I cannot say that this is the rope, but this is the kind of rope we used.

Q. Examine this rope and see whether it has probably been in use.

A. I cannot say. I cannot swear to it.

Q. Can you not say whether it has been probably in use at all?

A. This rope has been in use. That I know

from its appearance. It would have been lighter than this in color if it had not been used. Using ropes colors them.

Q. Can you tell anything as to whether the rope has been used or not by its flexibility?

A. I cannot; I have not sufficient acquaintance with ropes to tell anything of the kind. This is like the kind of rope we generally use in the flies—the rope we use for drawing up the different borders—what are called borders; that go across from one side of the wing to the other. It looks like a rope of that kind. This is a rope which has evidently been used from its color.

JOHN T. FORD,

a witness called for the accused, Edward Spangler, being duly sworn, testified as follows:

By Mr. EWING:

Q. State where you reside?

A. In the city of Baltimore.

Q. State whether or not you are the proprietor of Ford's Theatre in the city of Washington?

A. I am.

Q. State whether you are acquainted with the prisoner, Edward Spangler?

A. I am.

Q. How long has he been in your employ?

A. I think between three and four years at intervals; but over two years continuously.

Q. State whether or not you were in or about the theatre. or in this city, at the time of the assassination of President Lincoln.

A. I was not. I was in the city of Richmond on Friday, the day of the assassination; I arrived there about two o'clock.

Q. Were you acquainted with John Wilkes Booth?

A. I had known him since early childhood; I suppose since he was ten or eleven years of age; intimately for six or seven years. I saw him as a child frequently.

Q. State whether you have ever heard Booth speak of Samuel K. Chester, and if so, in what connection and where?

Assistant Judge Advocate BINGHAM. I object to any proof about what he said in regard to Chester.

Q. [By Mr. EWING.] State whether or not Booth ever applied to you to employ Chester, who has been a witness for the prosecution, in your theatre?

Assistant Judge Advocate BINGHAM. That I object to. It is certainly not competent to introduce declarations of Booth made to anybody in the absence of a witness that may be called; relative to a transaction of his, to affect him in any way at all. I object to it as wholly incompetent.

Mr. EWING. It is not to attack Chester, may it please the Court, that I make this inquiry, but rather to corroborate him; to show that Booth, while manipulating Chester to induce him to go into a conspiracy for the capture of the President, was actually at the same time endeavoring to induce Mr. Ford to employ Chester, in order that he might get him here to the theatre and use him as an instrument; and it goes to affect the case of several prisoners at the bar; the case of the prisoner, Arnold, who in his confession, as orally detailed here, stated that the plan was to capture the President, and Chester corroborates that; and also to assist the case of, the prisoner, Spangler, by showing that Booth was not able to get or did not get in the theatre any instruments to assist him in the purpose and was endeavoring to get them brought there—men that he has previously manipulated. I think it is legitimate.

Assistant Judge Advocate BINGHAM. Nothing can be clearer, if the Court please, than that it is utterly incompetent. It is not a simple question of relevancy here; it is absolute incompetency. A party who conspires to do a crime may approach the most upright man in the world with whom he has been, before the criminality was known to the world, on terms of intimacy, and whose position in the world was such that he might be on terms of intimacy with reputable gentlemen. It is the misfortune of a man that is approached in that way; it is not his crime, and it is not colorably his crime either. It does not follow now, because Booth chose to approach this man Chester, that Booth is therefore armed with the power, living or dead, to come into a court of justice and prove on his own motion, or on the motion of anybody else, what he may have said touching that man to third persons. The law is too jealous of the reputation and character of men to permit any such dealings at all.

The COMMISSION sustained the objection.

Q. [By Mr. EWING.] State what were the duties of the accused, Edward Spangler, on the stage.

A. Spangler was employed as a stage hand, frequently misrepresented as the stage-carpenter of the theatre. He was a laborer to assist in the shoving of scenery into its place, and removing it within the grooves as the necessity of the play required. These were his duties at night, and during the day to assist in doing the rough carpenter work incidental to plays to be produced.

Q. State whether or not his duties were such as to require his presence upon the stage during the whole of a play.

A. Strictly so. His absence for a moment might imperil the success of a play, and cause dissatisfaction to the audience. It is very important to the effect of a play that the scenery should be well attended to in all its changes; and he is absolutely important there every moment from the time the curtain rises until it falls. There are intervals, it is true, but he cannot judge how long or how brief a scene may be.

Q. State whether his constant presence during the second scene of the third act of the "American Cousin" would be necessary.

A. It would, unless he was positively informed of the duration of that scene. It is rather a long scene—longer perhaps than any other scene in that act.

Q. How is it with the first scene of the third act?

A. It is quick—but a few moments. The other is eight, or ten, or probably twelve minutes long.

Q. How is it with the second act?

A. The duration of a scene, I should say, depends very much on the action of the parties engaged in it—the spirit of the actors. Sometimes it is much more rapid than others. In the second act, I hardly think there is an interval between the time when he would move the scenes of more than five or eight minutes—between those numbers, I should say.

Q. His constant presence upon the stage, therefore, during the second act, throughout it, would be necessary?

A. Absolutely, if he attended to his duties.

Q. What were his duties in the intervals between the scenes?

A. To be prepared for the next change; to be ready at his scene; to remain on the side where the stage-carpenter had assigned him as his post of duty. Emergencies often arise during an act that require extra service of a stage.hand.

Q. State who had the regulation and control of the passage-way through which Booth escaped.

A. The stage manager directs, the stage carpenter executes the work belonging to that part of the theatre and to the entire stage.

Q. State who they were.

A. John B Wright was the stage manager, James J. Gifford the stage carpenter.

Q. Has not Gifford some subordinate who is charged with the duty of keeping the passage-way in its proper condition?

A. None except his stage hands. It is the duty of each and every one; it is as indispensable as keeping the front door clear. The action of the play would be ruined by any obstruction or incumbrance there.

Q. The stage hands on which side of the theatre?

A. Of course, on the side where this passage is.

Q That is the side opposite to the one on which Spangler worked?

A. I presumed you meant what we call the prompt side, the side on which the prompter is located, the chief passage of the theatre; Spangler worked on the other side. The stage carpenter's place was to be on this side, but we frequently do not require actual work by him; he manages the scenery, but leaves it to the stage hands to work the scenes unless there is a difficult play. His location is near the stage manager, to receive his directions and to be subordinate to him.

Q. And the two are located on the stage, on the side opposite to that where the prisoner, Spangler, worked upon?

A. Directly opposite. They are on the prompt side; he on the O. P. side—opposite the prompt place.

Q. Then I understand that the prisoner, Spangler, would not be charged with the duty of keeping that passage-way in order?

A. That was no duty of his, unless specially assigned to him by the stage carpenter; he was subordinate entirely to the stage carpenter.

Q. Now state whether or not that passage-way is generally obstructed in any way.

A. It should never be obstructed. My positive orders are to keep it always clear and in the best order. It is the passage-way used by all the parties coming from the dressing-rooms. Where a play was performed like the "American Cousin" the ladies were in full dress, and it was absolutely necessary that there should be no obstruction there, in order that the play should be properly performed. Coming from the dressing-rooms and the green-room of the theatre every one had to use that passage. The other side of the stage was not used more than a third as much, probably. Most of the entrances by the actors and actresses are made on the prompt side; but many are essential to be made on the O. P. side. By entrances to the stage, I mean to the presence of the audience.

Q. Do you know whether as a matter of fact that passage-way was kept by the stage manager clear?

A. The stage manager was a very exacting man in all those details, and I have always found it clear, unless there was some spectacular play in which he required the whole spread of the stage. Then at times it would be partly encumbered, but not enough so to prevent the people going around the stage or going to the cellar-way and underneath and passing to the other side by way of the cellar.

Q. Was the "American Cousin" such a spectacular play?

A. No, it was a very plain play; no obstruction whatever could be excused on account of that play; it was all what we call flats. except one scene; the flats are the large scenes that cross the stage.

Q. Did you ever see the prisoner, Edward Spangler, wear a moustache?

A. Never.

Q. State his relations to Booth, as far as you have known them to be together at all.

A. He seemed to have a great admiration for Booth. I have noticed that, in my business on the stage with the stage manager. Booth was a peculiarly fascinating man, and controlled the lower class of people, such as Spangler belonged to, I suppose more than ordinary men would—a man who excelled in all manly sports.

Q. Was Spangler at all in the employment of Booth?

A. Not to my knowledge.

Q. Was he in the habit of waiting upon him?

A. I only heard so; I never knew, until after the assassination, that he had been so employed.

Q. State to the Court whether or not, from your knowledge of Booth, the leap from the box upon the stage would be a difficult one.

A. By no means, I think. He excelled in everything of that kind. He had a reputation for being a great gymnast. He introduced, in some Shaksperian plays, some of the most extraordinary and outrageous leaps, deemed so by the critics and condemned by the press at the time.

Q. Did you ever see him make any of those extraordinary leaps?

A. I did on one occasion, and the Baltimore Sun condemned it in an editorial the next day—styled him the "gymnastic actor." It was in the play of Macbeth, the entrance to the witch scene; he jumped from a high rock down on the stage, as high or perhaps higher than the box; I think about as high, nearly, as from the top of the scene.

Q. You think, then, from your knowledge of the physical powers of Booth, that that leap was one that he would not need to rehearse?

A. I would not think a rehearsal of it was needed. He was a very bold, fearless man; he always had the reputation of being of that character. I should not suppose any rehearsal would be necessary. We never rehearse leaps in the theatre, even when they are necessary to the action of the play; they may be gone over the first time a play is performed, but it is not usual.

Q Do you think that leap from the President's box upon the stage would be at all a difficult one for Booth?

A. I should not think so; I have seen him make a similar leap without any hesitation, and I am aware that he usually introduced it in the play of Macbeth, as I stated before.

Q. Did he make the leap of which you speak with ease?

A. Apparently; without any hesitation, at least; no effect following it

Q. State whether you have any knowledge as to Booth's frequenting Ford's Theatre.

A. I seldom visited the theatre but what I found him about or near it, during the day, while I was there. I usually came down to the theatre three days a week, devoting the other three to my business in Baltimore, and being there between the hours of ten and three, I would nearly always meet Booth there when he was in the city. He had his letters directed to the theatre, and that was the cause of his frequent visits there, as I thought then.

Q. During what period was that?

A. Nearly the entire season; which commenced about the 1st of September—say from the latter part of September up to the time I saw him last in Washington.

Q. When was that last time you saw him?

A. Some two or three weeks before the assination. Just previous to the assassination my wife was in bad health, and I was not down here as frequently as I had been before.

Q. Can you State whether or not you were here about the 2d of April? .

A. I could not positively, without some reflection. It is hard to locate a date precisely. I usually came down here on Mondays, Wednesdays, and Fridays, but sometimes it was on Tuesdays, Thursday, and Saturdays. I cannot say positive that I was here on the day named.

Q. Do you know where the actor John McCullough was then?

A. In New York, or at least he ought to have been there. Mr. Forrest was acting there and he always appears in his plays. His last appearance at my theatre was the 18th of March; that, I believe, was the night the Apostate was played, and his last service in the theatre. Mr. Forrest was within a week to appear in New York, and he accompanied him.

Q. State whether or not you know anything of the prisoner, Spangler, having been in the habit of going to Baltimore, and for what, during the spring.

A. I know that he had lived in Baltimore and buried his wife there some eight or ten months, or probably a year ago, whilst in my employ, and that he considered Baltimore his home, and usually spent the summer months, during the vacation of the theatre, there, chiefly in crabbing and fishing. He was a great fisher and crabber. I know nothing positive of my own knowledge as to that. I only heard that, and we used to plague him about it.

Q. [Exhibiting to witness the coil of rope found in a carpet bag at the house where Spangler took his meals.] Look at that rope and see whether or not it might be used for any such purpose, and in what way.

A. I suppose that could be used as a crab line, though it is rather short for that purpose.

Q. Explain to the Court how it could be used.

A. I have seen them catch crabs with a long rope, and with smaller ropes or lines appended to it, which they fixed to it. The ropes are supported by buoys; they spread them out to catch crabs. The professional crabbers use much longer ropes than this—those who make a business of it.

Q. What length of rope have you seen used in that sport?

A. Four or five hundred feet.

Q. Have you seen shorter ropes than that used?

A. I have seen some as short used. I have read that the length of this is eighty feet, but I do not know from its appearance.

Q. This is such a rope as you have seen used by amateurs in that sport?

A. Yes, sir; I have seen such ropes. I frequently go fishing in the summer.

Q. State to the Court what your object was in going to Richmond about the time of the assassination of the President of the United States.

 A. I had there an uncle, a very aged man, and a mother-in-law, the mother of my wife, and hearing of the partial destruction of Richmond by fire, I went there anxious to ascertain their condition. I arrived their on Friday. I did not hear of the assassination until Sunday night; and then I heard that Edwin Booth was charged with it. On Saturday morning my uncle, the only male blood relative I found there, went up with me to take the oath of allegiance. On Sunday I spent the day with him, and on Monday morning I started for Baltimore and Washington by the six o'clock boat, and at the boat I first saw the Richmond Whig, which confirmed the report I had heard on Sunday night of the assassination. I was in company, while at Richmond, with Col. Forney and others, conferring with them, at times, in regard to people I had known there when I lived there for three or four years from 1850.

Cross-examined by the JUDGE ADVOCATE:

Q. You do not mean to state to this Court that the prisoner, Spangler, intended to catch crabs with that rope which was shown to you?

A. No, sir.

Q. That rope could be used quite as well for other purposes as for catching crabs?

A. Unquestionable. I have no doubt of that.

Q. State whether or not the private boxes in your theatre, of which the President occupied one, are ordinarially kept locked when not in actual use?

A. I cannot state that positively. I did not spend a great many nights in Washington. In Baltimore we always keep the private boxes locked.

Q. Who has the custody of those boxes during the day, when they are not actually occupied?

A. The stage carpenter, Mr. Gifford, had control of the whole theatre, and would be the responsible party I should blame for anything wrong about the boxes.

Q. You cannot state. therefore, whether they were locked or not?

A. No, sir. In Baltimore we keep them locked, and keep the keys in the box office where we sell the boxes to patrons. Here I understand that the ushers retained the keys.

Q. Who was the usher in this building?

A. The chief usher was James O'Brien, the usher of the dress circle and of the boxes on that tier.

Q. Do you know who had for sale the tickets for those boxes that day?

A. Yes, sir; the authorized parties were my two brothers, James R. and Henry Clay Ford.

Q Do you know the fact that none of the boxes were occupied that night except that occupied by the President?

A. I have only heard so.

Q. Is the play of the "American Cousin" a popular one? Does it attract considerable audiences?

A. It was, when originally produced, an exceedingly attractive play; of late years it has not been a strong card, but a fair attraction.

Q. Is it not a very unusual thing, when such plays are produced, for your private boxes to be entirely empty?

A. Washington is a very good place for selling boxes usually. They are generally in demand, and nearly always two or three boxes are sold.

Q. Can you recall any occasion on which a play so popular and attractive as that was presented when none of your private boxes, save the one occupied by the President, was used?

A. I remember occasions when we sold no boxes at all, and had quite a full house—a good audience; but those occasions were rare. My reason for constructing so many boxes to this theatre was that usually private boxes were in demand in Washington more so than in almost any other city. It is not a favorable place to see a performance, but it is a fashionable place here to take company.

Q. Did I understand you to say that from the character of the two men, and their relations to each other, as known to you, Booth would be likely to exert a large influence over the prisoner, Spangler?

A. I think he would, over men of that class that he came in contact with.

Q. Either for good or evil, as it might chance to be?

A. Yes, sir.

By the Court:

Q. State the size of the rope usually used as a crab-rope?

A. I merely know the length of the rope I have seen here.

Q. Give the dimensions of it, the width around, by the usual rule of measurement?

A. I have rather a bad eye for size. I suppose this rope is nearly an inch round in circumference.

Q. Is it at least an inch?

A. I should think so.

J. P. FERGUSON

recalled for the accused Edward Spangler.

By Mr. Ewing:

Q. State to the Court whether, directly after the assassination of the President, you saw Mr. Stewart get upon the stage.

A. I am not personally acquainted with Mr. Stewart; do not know that I know the gen-

tleman at all; I saw a gentleman, the first one who got upon the stage after Booth passed off. He was a large man, dressed in light clothes, with a moustache. I do not know whether it was Mr. Stewart or not. A moment after he jumped on the stage, Miss Harris called, up in the President's box, for water. I saw that man turn around and look up towards the box at a soldier who was on guard there, running plump up. Some one halloed, "catch him." Laura Keene came in at the corner at the entrance right directly under where I sat, and she raised both hands and said, "We have got him," or "We will get him." By that time there were, I suppose half a dozen men on the stage. I then saw this large man run out by Laura Keene, at the side entrance, in the direction that Booth had taken. He was the first one to get on the stage

Q. Could you describe the color of his hair?

A. I could not. He was a large man; I suppose as tall as I am, and heavier. He had on light clothes, and a moustache. He was the first one that got on the stage. I should suppose it was probably two or three minutes —about that long—after Booth went off the stage that this man went out of the entrance.

Q. Had you seen anybody else run out of the entrance?

A. No person but Hawk, the young man who was on the stage at the time Booth jumped from the box.

Q. If any one had run out of the entrance, following Booth, would you probably have seen him?

A. I would, because I thought it very singular that those who were near the stage did not try to run and get on it. I know that if I had occupied the position some of them did, I would have got on the stage. I am not acquainted with Mr. Stewart, and would not know him now if I were to see him.

By Assistant Judge Advocate Bingham:

Q. You sat in the gallery all the time of this transaction?

A. In the dress circle.

Q. On which side of the dress circle did you sit, the north or the south side?

A. I sat on the north side.

Q. And the entrance that you were talking about, through which the parties passed, was on the north side of the stage, too?

A. Yes, sir.

Q. How near did you sit to the private boxes on the north side of the gallery?

A. I was very close to the private boxes.

Q. Then you could not see the mouth of the entrance distinct'y from where you sat?

A. No, sir, not exactly from where I sat; I could not see it distinctly. I saw Laura Keene come on, and run in.

Q. And you cannot say what persons passed between the various scenes into the general entrance at all?

A. There might have been such a thing.

Q. And you cannot say anything about that?

A. This large man was the first one that jumped on the stage.

By Mr. Ewing:

Q. Had the man any other whisker beside a moustache?

A. I do not think he had, but I will not be positive; he might have had.

C. D. HESS,

a witness called for the accused, Edward Spangler, being duly sworn, testified as follows:

By Mr. Ewing:

Q. State your business here in Washington.

A. I am the manager of Grover's Theatre.

Q. Is that a theatre rival to Ford's?

A. It is so considered. I believe.

Q. State whether you were in the habit of seeing John Wilkes Booth during the last season before the assassination of the President.

A. Yes, sir, very frequently.

Q. State whether he ever made any inquiry of you in regard to the President's attending your theatre.

A. He did make such an inquiry.

Q. When?

A. On the day before the assassination.

Q. State the circumstances under which the inquiry was made.

A. He came into the office some time during the afternoon, I think, of Thursday, interrupted me and the prompter of the theatre in reading a manuscript, seated himself in a chair and entered into conversation on the subject of the illumination. There was to be a general illumination of the city on Thursday night, and he asked me if I intended to illuminate. I told him yes, I would illuminate to a certain extent that night, but that the next night would be my great night of the illumination, that being the celebration of the fall of Sumter. He asked me the question—my impression is his words were, "Do you intend" or "Are you going to invite the President?" I think my reply was, "Yes; that reminds me I must send that invitation." I had had it in my mind for several days to invite the Presidential party down on that night—on the night of the 14th.

Q. Did you invite the President?

A. I sent Mrs. Lincoln an invitation. My notes were usually addressed to her as the best means of accomplishing the object.

Q. Of getting the President there?

A. Yes, sir.

Q. That was on what day?

A. On Thursday—the day before the assassination.

Q. And the invitation was for that night?

A. For the following night, the night of the assassination.

Q. Was there anything marked in Booth's manner in making this inquiry of you?

A. It struck me as rather peculiar, his entering in the manner that he did; he must have observed that we were busy, and it was not usual for him to come in and take a seat unless he was invited. He did upon that occasion, and made such a point of it that we were both considerably surprised. He pushed the matter so far that I got up and put the manuscript away and entered into conversation with him.

Q. Did he or did he not, on any occasion before that, solicit you to invite the President?

A. Not to my recollection.

Q. Were you in the habit of seeing him frequently?

A. Very frequently.

Q. State whether or not it is customary in theatres to keep the passage-way between the scenes and the green-room and the dressing room clear.

A. Yes, sir, that is a point of excellence in a stage carpenter. If he keeps a clean stage and his scenes well put away, the passages as clear as possible, we look upon him as a careful man. It depends entirely on how much room they have, however, for storing scenes.

Q. What is usually the width of the passage-way between the scenes and those rooms?

A. I do not know of any two theatres in the country alike in that respect. It depends entirely on the construction of the building.

Would you consider three and a half feet a wide or a narrow passage?

A. I should consider it rather narrow.

Q. Would it or not be more necessary to keep it clear if the passage-way were narrow?

A. Decidedly so.

Q. You have been in Ford's Theatre?

A. Yes, sir; I have been in the theatre.

Q. You know about the height of the second tier of boxes from the stage?

A. Yes, sir; I do from general observation only.

Q. Would you consider the leap from the second tier of boxes to the stage an extraordinary or difficult one?

A. From my present recollection I should say not very difficult.

Q. State what box the President was in the habit of occupying when he attended your theatre.

A. We have two communicating boxes on the right hand side of the theatre, on the stage floor, the lower floor—

Assistant Judge Advocate Bingham. We do not care anything about inquiring into the condition of Grover's Theatre here. It is only a waste of time.

Mr. Ewing. More time is wasted by objecting to it. I must insist on the question.

Assistant Judge Advocate Bingham. I object to it because it has nothing to do with the issue. We have introduced no evidence here touching any transaction in Grover's Theatre. It is Ford's Theatre that is before this Court. He purposes to go into a minute inquiry, I suppose, of all about Grover's Theatre, and how it is built, how its stage is constructed, its scenes, boxes, its avenues of approach, &c. I do not want to be delayed here with any such inquiry. I do not care anything about the structure of that building.

Mr. Ewing. I wish no very minute inquiry in regard to Grover's Theatre; I merely wish to show the Court that from the construction of Ford's Theatre, it would be easier for a man who sought to assassinate the President to escape after having committed the crime than it would be to escape from Grover's Theatre, had he committed the crime there. The purpose of it is very plain, to show why Ford's Theatre was selected by Booth, why Ford's Theatre is spoken of as having been the one where Booth intended to capture or assassinate the President, for the purpose of relieving the employees of Ford's Theatre, and Mr. Spangler among them, from the imputation which naturally arises from the fact that Booth had selected that theatre as the one at which he intended to commit the crime.

Assistant Judge Advocate BINGHAM. It is very apparent that nobody can be responsible for any act of Booth, unless by his own voluntary act he assented to it; and the introduction of proof, therefore, about Grover's Theatre can neither excuse nor tend to excuse any man connected with Ford's Theatre for any act of his; and unless we prove the act of somebody at Ford's Theatre, they are not responsible for it, of course. But the attempt here is to prove the structure of Grover's Theatre, and that it is not as well adapted to assassination as Ford's; that is about the amount of it. I do not want to be delayed here with any inquiries about Grover's Theatre.

The PRESIDENT. I do not think the Court need vote on that if the Judge Advocate objects to it. The question is evidently improper and the Court so decides.

Mr. Ewing. I ask for a decision by the Commission.

The COMMISSION sustained the objection.

HENRY M. JAMES,

witness called for the accused, Edward Spangler, being duly sworn, testified as follows:

By Mr. Ewing:

Q. State whether you are acquainted with the prisoner Edward Spangler.

A. Yes, sir; I have been for a short time.

Q. Were you in Ford's Theatre when the President was assassinated?

A. I was.

Q. State your position and the position of Edward Spangler, if you know what it was, at that time.

A. I was standing ready to draw off the flat, and Mr. Spangler was standing right opposite to me on the stage at the time it happened.

Q. You heard the shot fired?

A. Yes, sir.

Q. From the position you were in, you could not then see the President's box?

A. I could not. There was a flat between me and the President.

Q. From the position Spangler was in, could he see it?

A. No, sir.

Q. Could he see the front part of the stage on which Booth jumped?

A. No, sir. He was standing behind the scene.

Q. On which side of the centre of the stage? —on the side towards that on which the President's box was?

A. Mr. Spangler was on the side towards the President's box.

Q. And was he in position to draw off the flat on the side opposite to you?

A. Yes, sir. He was standing right close alongside of it.

Q. Did you see any one standing by him?

A. I did not.

Q. When the shot was fired, did you see what he did?

A. I did not.

Q. Did you notice whether he moved away or remained?

A. I did not.

Q. What did you do yourself?

A. I hardly know what I did. I did as the rest of them did, looked around. I was excited at the time. I did not go anywhere. I just stayed where I was at, standing right behind the curtain.

Q. How far was Spangler from you?

A. I judge he was about ten feet. I do not know exactly, but I judge about that.

Q. Which was nearer to the door out of which Booth ran—you or Spangler?

A. I was nearest to it, I judge.

Q. How much nearer?

A. I cannot say. There was but very little difference.

Q. Did you see anybody near Spangler at that time?

A. I did not.

Q. Had you seen him previously during the play?

A. I had often seen him every time there was anything to do there; I did not notice him any other time, only when the scenes had to be changed I saw him there at his post.

Q. What was the condition of the passageway at that time; was it clear?

A. Yes, sir; it was clear.

Q. How should it have been?

A. It should have been kept clear; that was our place to keep it clear; that is what we were there for.

Q. Whose business was it particularly to see that it was clear?

A. It was mine and Spangler's to keep the passage clear.

Q. Was it more your business than Spangler's?

A. It was more Spangler's business.

Q. Was not the passage on your side?

A. Yes, sir.

Q. And it was part of your business to keep it clear?

A. It was part of my business to keep it clear.

Q. Did you see Spangler when the President entered the theatre?

A. I saw him standing on the opposite side from me when the President entered.

Q. Did you see him at the time of the applause which followed the President's entry occurred?

A. I did; and he applauded with them.

Q. How?

A. Loud, with his hands and feet both; clapped his hands and stamped his feet; seemed as pleased as anybody to see the President come in.

Q. Did you see anything of Jacob Ritterspaugh near Spangler that night?

A. I did not. He might have been there behind some of the scenes; I did not notice him.

Q. He was not out of your view?

A. No, sir; not at the time it happened.

Q. How long did you stay where you were after it happened?

A. I do not recollect. I might have stood there half a minute—maybe a minute—I cannot say, in the excitement.

Q. Did you hear Spangler say anything at that time?

A. I did not. I did not see Spangler after it happened at all.

Q. Did he go away?

A. I do not know.

By Assistant Judge Advocate BINGHAM:

Q. Jacob Ritterspaugh, you say, might have been there behind the scenes, and you not have seen him?

A. He might have been.

Q. He was employed there at the time?

A. Yes, sir.

Q. It was his business to be there?

A. Yes, sir.

By Mr. EWING:

Q. His business to be where?

A. Behind the scenes.

THOMAS J. RAYBOLD,

recalled for the accused, Edward Spangler.

By Mr. EWING:

Q. Have you since you were upon the stand to-day visited Ford's theatre?

A. I have.

Q. Have you examined the keepers of the locks of boxes 7 and 8?

A. Yes, sir.

Q. State the condition in which you found the locks of those boxes.

A. Box 8—the box that I this morning testified to forcing—is in the condition that I stated. It has been forced, and the wood has been split by forcing the lock. Box 7 has been forced, and you can take the screws out with your finger and push it in and out.—Both have been forced, but I was not aware of it. I knew nothing about them, except the one I testified to, until I saw them there now.

Q. Did you ascertain the condition of the screws in the keeper in box 8?

A. Only from what I saw when I was there to-day. The screw in the keeper of box 8 is tight; the keeper has been drawn around, and you have to twist it to get it around. But in the other box the keeper has been forced, and the upper screw can be drawn out without any difficulty; you can put your thumb against it and push it to the full extent of the screw.

Q. But the wood into which the screws of the keeper of box 8 were screwed is split?

A. Yes, sir, that is split; the screw is not drawn; the keeper is forced aside—a thing that would be done by force. It is forced aside, it is not completly pushed out.

Q. Could you say, from your examination, whether or not that had been done by any instrument?

A. I cannot say as to an instrument. It must have been done by force; I know that one was, and the other has every appearance of it.

Q. By force applied to the outside of the doors?

A. Yes, sir.

By Assistant Judge Advocate BINGHAM:

Q. You say the wood in box 7 is not split?

A. Not a particle.

Q. What is the reason you say it has every appearance of having been forced from the outside?

A. If a screw was drawn by a screw-driver, when it went back again it would have to be put back by a driver; but when force has been used you can put it in or out.

Q. If an instrument had been used, would it not probably have left it so that it would work just as it does work?

A. Yes, sir, anybody could draw a screw out and put anything else in; but then it would make a hole much larger.

By Mr. EWING:

Q. In forcing the lock, if the screws were forced out straight, they would tear the wood would it not?

A. Yes, sir.

Q. It would enlarge the hole?

A. They would not be so apt to come all the way out; you could pull them out, but they would still be fast.

By Mr. AIKEN:

Q. Did you know John H. Surratt?

A. No, sir; I do not know any of them [pointing to the prisoners] except Spangler; he is the only one of them I ever saw, that I know of, except one, whom I knew when he was quite a boy.

JOSEPH T. K. PLANT,

a witness called for the accused, Edward Spangler, being duly sworn, testified as follows:

By Mr. EWING:

Q. State your residence and occupation.

A. My occupation is that of a dealer in furniture at present. My trade is that of a paper-hanger. My residence is 350 D street, between Ninth and Tenth streets, in Washington.

Q. Have you been engaged, at any time, in cabinet work?

A. Ever since I was about fourteen years old, more or less.

Q. State whether or not you have visited Ford's Theatre to-day.

A. I have.

Q. State whether you examined the keepers of the locks on any of the private boxes; if so, what ones, and what condition you found them in.

A. I examined the keepers on boxes 7 and 8. To all appearances they had both been forced. The woodwork in box 8 is shivered and splintered by the screws. In box 7 I could pull the screw with my thumb and finger; the tap was gone clear to the point. I could force it back with my thumb. In box 4, which is directly under box 8, the keeper is gone entirely.

Q. State whether or not, according to your professional opinion, the keepers of the locks in boxes 7 and 8 were made loose by an instrument or by force applied to the outside of the doors.

A. I should judge by force.

Q. Is there any appearance of an instrument having been used to draw the screws in either of those boxes?

A. I could see no such evidence.

Q. You say the wood into which the screws of box 8 go is splintered?

A. Yes, sir.

Q. Apparently by pressure from without against the door?

A. I should so suppose. According to my judgment, it was done by that means.

Q. State whether you noticed a hole in the wall in the passage which leads behind the boxes

A. Yes, sir.

Q. State whether that hole has any appearance of having been covered?

A. It certainly has been covered with a piece of something, I could not say what, because there has been no remnant of it left.

Q. How large a piece?

A. I did not charge my memory exactly with that, but I should suppose about five by

seven and a half or eight inches in size, an oblong piece.

Q. Did you notice a hole in the door of either of those two boxes?

A. There is a hole in the door of box 7.

Q. What sized hole?

A. A little more than a quarter of an inch in diameter. It is larger on the outside, I think, than it is on the inside, a sort of wedge-shaped.

Q. Could you tell how that had been made?

A. I should judge it was made with some instrument. One part of it felt to me as if shaved by a knife.

Q. Which side was that?

A. At the right hand of the door and at the bottom of the hole, on the outside of the moulding.

Q. Did any part of it look as if it had been made by a gimlet?

That is a hard question to answer. There is one part of the hole, to the left, which feels rough, as if cut by a gimlet, or caused by the working of a gimlet after the hole was bored; but the lower part of it, on the right hand side, appears to have been trimmed by a penknife, or some sharp instrument of that kind.

Q. Do you think, then, a gimlet was used in making the hole?

A. Something of that sort, or it might have been made by a penknife, and the roughness might have been caused by the back of the knife.

JOSEPH S. SESSFORD,

a witness called for the accused, Edward Spangler, being duly sworn, testified as follows:

By Mr. EWING:

Q. State the business you were employed in on the 14th of April last?

A. I was ticket seller at Ford's Theatre.

Q. How long were you at the ticket office, during the day or night?

A. My business commenced at about half past six o'clock in the evening.

Q State whether any of the private boxes, except those occupied by the party of the President, were applied for during that evening?

A. No, sir.

Q. Had any of the tickets for those boxes been sold during the day?

A. I think not.

L. A. GOBRIGHT,

a witness called for the accused, Edward Spangler, being duly affirmed, testified as follows:

By Mr. EWING:

Q. State in what business you have been engaged in Washington city for the past six or eight months?

A. My business is connected with the press.

My profession is that of a journalist, a reporter, and telegraphic correspondent.

Q. Of the Associated Press?

A. Yes, sir.

Q. Will you state whether you were at Ford's Theatre after the assassination of the President on Friday night, the 14th of April?

A. I was.

Q. What did you learn there as to who was the assassin? Did you learn positively who it was?

A. I heard some persons say positively that it was Wilkes Booth; and others said that they knew Wilkes Booth, but the man who jumped upon the stage and made his exit differed somewhat in appearance from Wilkes Booth. There did not seem to be any certainty, so far as I could ascertain at that time.

Q. How long was that after the assassination?

A. I was informed of the assassination, I suppose, about twenty minutes to eleven o'clock, and I arrived at the theatre at five minutes to eleven that night.

Q. State whether you became certain that night who it was that had killed the President?

A. I was not positively satisfied on that occasion, during that visit which I made to the theatre, in my own mind, who was the assassin.

Cross-examined by Assistant Judge Advocate BINGHAM:

Q. You did become satisfied during that night that Wilkes Booth had killed the President?

A. I was not perfectly satisfied of that fact.

Q. But during the night you were?

A. Not thoroughly satisfied.

Q. You were so satisfied that night anyhow that you came to the conclusion that Wilkes Booth was probably the man, and so telegraphed to the country?

A. I did not telegraph that fact.

Q. It was telegraphed?

A. It was telegraphed that night; I could tell by whom if necessary.

Q. You came to the conclusion very suddenly next morning that Wilkes Booth was the man?

A. After I saw the official bulletin the next morning.

JUNE 13.

J. L. DEBONAY,

was recalled for the accused, Edward Spangler.

By Mr. EWING:

Q State to the Court again where you were standing when the shot was fired in the theatre on the night of the 14th of April.

A. I was standing on the left-hand side, first entrance.

Q. You mean the side the President's box was on?

A. Yes, sir.

Q. How long was it, after you saw Mr. Stewart run out after Booth, before you saw the accused, Edward Spangler; and where did you see him, and what did you see him do?

A. The first time I saw him, he was moving his scene, I think. They shoved the scene back to give the whole of the stage to the people who came on. I do not know who assisted him.

Q How long was that after Mr. Stewart had left the stage?

A. I guess it was about a minute and a half or two minutes.

Q. Was it long enough for Mr. Stewart to have got out of the back door?

A I think he had just about time to get to the back door before they shoved the scenes.

Q. What did Spangler do then?

A. He came in front on the stage, with the rest There was a cry for water, and I started to the green room, and he started the same way. About half a dozen of us went to get some water to carry it to the private box.

Q. How far did Spangler go after the water? Did he go into the green-room?

A. We all went into the green-room; about a half a dozen of us went into the green-room. By that time the stage was full of people.

Q Did you see anything of Mr. Sleickman when Booth said he wanted Spangler to hold his horse and you went over for Spangler?

A. They were both standing at the same place, very near, close to each other, on the opposite side of the stage.

Q. That is on the left hand side of the stage looking to the audience?

A. Yes, sir; and the same side that the President's box was on.

Q. Did Mr. Sleickman go over to the door?

A. I did not see him go over there.

Did you see Spangler go over?

A. Yes, sir; because I went right behind him, pretty close.

Q. Did you see Spangler go out of the door?

A. Yes, sir.

Q. Did you see Booth then come in?

A. I did.

Q. How long was it after Spangler went out before Booth came in?

A. About a minute, or a minute and a half —not longer than that.

Q. How far were you from the door?

A. I was about halfway between the back door and the green-room—about eighteen or twenty feet, I suppose.

Q. Did you hear any conversation between Spangler and Booth?

A. I did not.

Q. Did you hear anything to indicate that there was conversation going on between them?

A. No, sir.

Q. Did Booth meet Spangler inside of the door?

A. He was standing at the door; he was on the outside. The door was about half open when Spangler went out.

Q. Would you have seen any person who followed Spangler, and went out, too?

A. Yes, sir; I think I should have seen any one.

Q. And you did not see Stoickman?

A. I did not.

Q. When Booth came in, what did he do?

A. He went under the stage to the opposite side, and he went out the side door.

Q. How do you know that he went out the side door?

A. Because I went under the stage and crossed to the opposite side myself.

Q. Did you go under with Booth?

A. Yes, sir, I went under with him.

Q. And he went out of the side-door?

A. Yes.

Q. Did he have any conversation with any one?

A. Not to my knowledge. I did not see him speak to any person.

Q. Were you on the pavement in front of the theatre shortly before the assassination?

A. I was on the pavement about five minutes before it occurred.

Q. Did you see Spangler in front there?

A. I did not.

Q. Did you ever see Spangler at any time wear a moustache?

A. I have seen him wear a kind of rough whiskers, or rather unshaved. I never noticed particularly about a moustache.

Q. Did you ever see him wear a heavy moustache?

A. No, sir, I never did see him wear a heavy moustache while I was there, and that was about six months.

Q. You knew Spangler well?

A. Yes, sir.

Q. Was he a man who would likely to be entrusted with the secrets of others?

A. I do not know. I cannot tell. He is a man that was a little dissipated a big portion of the time, fond of sprecing around, and I should not think a person would be likely to trust him.

Q. How was he when in liquor? Was he inclined to be recreative or to talk much?

A. He was free in conversation, like a great many other persons, very free in talking.

Cross-examined by Assistant Judge Advocate BINGHAM:

Q. You say that Booth went out at the side-door after passing under the stage?

A. Yes, sir.

Q. Do you mean that he went through the side-passage, level with the lower floor of the theatre, into Tenth street?

A. Yes, sir.

Q. And you followed him through?

A. No, I did not follow him out there.

Q. How do you know he went out?

A. He went out the side-door; that is the passage.

Q. What became of him? Where did he go to?

A. I do not know.

Q. Where did he go to when he went out the side-door?

A. He must have gone out into Tenth street; that is the only way the passage leads.

Q. Could he not have gone from that same side-door out of which he passed, up to the rooms occupied by Ford?

A. Yes, sir, he could have gone up where, because there is a passage-way that leads up into Ford's room.

Q. You said you went out that way yourself?

A. No, I said I came up under the stage.

Q. But you said that you went out yourself by the side-door?

A. I was asked if I was in front of the theatre, and I said I was.

Q. Did you not say that you were in front of the theatre about five minutes before the President was shot?

A. Yes, sir.

Q. Did you not say that you got there by the side-door?

A. That is the way I went through.

Q. You went through by the side-door, along the little passage that is outside of the wall of the theatre, and out of the little narrow door that opens on Tenth street at the south side of the theatre?

A. Yes, sir.

Q. That is the way you went?

A. That is the way I went.

Q. Did you go back the same way?

A. I went back the same way into the theatre.

Q. And had taken your place on the stage when the pistol was fired?

A. Yes, sir.

Q. What were you doing when the pistol was fired?

A. I was not doing anything. I was standing, leaning up against the corner of the scene.

Q. Was anybody else doing anything when the pistol was fired?

A. They were waiting for the curtain to drop. Mr. Harry Hawk was on the stage at that moment, playing in a scene.

By Mr. EWING:

Q. Had you any part to play that night?

A. Yes, sir; I played a part in the piece called John Wigger, the gardener.

By Assistant Judge Advocate BURNETT:

Q. What were your duties at the theatre?

A. I was an actor there.

Q. What parts did you play?

A. What is called in the theatrical profession, "general utility" business—"responsible utility."

Index of Witnesses.

FOR THE PROSECUTION.

FOR THE DEFENCE.

This Evidence is Reprinted from the Official Court Record.